BLOOD
WILLOW

BLOOD WILLOW

THOMAS BLOOR

Hodder
Children's
Books

a division of Hodder Headline Limited

For Kate, Sarah and Rebecca

A Catalogue record for this book is available
from the British Library

ISBN 0 340 86647 0

Typeset in Palatino by Avon DataSet Ltd,
Bidford-on-Avon, Warwickshire

Printed and bound in Great Britain by
Bookmarque Ltd, Croydon, Surrey

Hodder Children's Books
a division of Hodder Headline Limited
338 Euston Road
London NW1 3BH

Contents

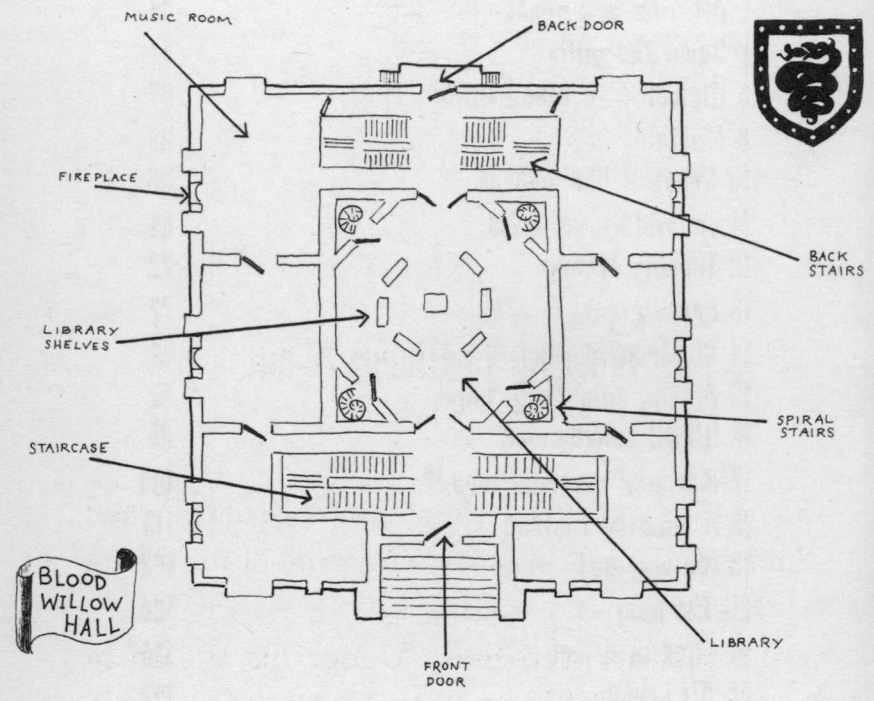

MUSIC ROOM

BACK DOOR

FIREPLACE

LIBRARY
SHELVES

STAIRCASE

BACK
STAIRS

SPIRAL
STAIRS

LIBRARY

FRONT
DOOR

BLOOD
WILLOW
HALL

1

Nothing to Worry About

Something moved beneath the surface of the water. Something big. It was heading straight for them.

"Basking shark," said Jack.

Rosh swallowed hard. Under his breath he began whispering everything he knew about basking sharks. "They grow big. Up to ten metres. You get them off the British coast. Their mouths are huge but they've got no teeth. They eat plankton. Microscopic stuff. We've got nothing to worry about. Nothing to worry about."

Rosh closed his eyes and, for a brief moment, he pictured his *Big Book of Sharks and Whales in Full Colour*. He had had it for years, a present from his Auntie Irene when he was little. It was on the shelf back home, up in his bedroom. He knew exactly where.

He pictured himself plucking it off the shelf, crossing over to his bed and collapsing on to the crumpled duvet. Curled up there, he could leaf through the old book, enjoying the familiar illustrations of hammerheads, makos and tiger sharks; of humpbacks, porpoises and killer whales; safe in the knowledge that he would never have to meet such a creature. One of the cats, probably Graham because Aravinda preferred to sleep at the top of the stairs, would be curled up on the pillow, purring loudly. It would be raining outside. A few drops would patter against the windowpane and Rosh would shiver happily, up in the quiet of his bedroom with the radiator on full.

But he was not at home. In fact, he was miles and miles away from London. He was far to the north east, somewhere off the Northumbrian coast, rolling on a heavy swell in a leaky canoe, with his cousin Jack sitting, stiff-backed and red-necked, in front of him. A thick bank of mist had settled on the water all around them and there was a big, dark shape just beneath the surface, now circling them with lazy determination.

Rosh was shivering all right, but he was not even remotely happy. The reality of the situation they were facing was hard to bear. He felt tears spring into his eyes and he tried to banish all thoughts of home, of his dad standing out in the kitchen, sipping from a mug of tea and listening to the radio, of his mum calling up the stairs when she put out the cat food; "Graham! Arry!" She would never call Arivinder by his full name. It was a Sri Lankan name and his mum never liked to think about Sri Lanka. Rosh had chosen the cats' names himself, one English, one Sri Lankan. They were names he had found in an old cricket magazine of his dad's, a name for his English dad and a name for his Sri Lankan mum.

Now here he was, like his mother, trying not to think about his home. But for very different reasons. He was also trying not to think about the story he had read in a newspaper a couple of years ago, about a Great White Shark, the most ferocious man-eater of them all, which had been spotted off the coast of Cornwall, only a few hundred miles away from where they were now. What were a few hundred miles to a seven-metre shark?

He felt a wave of anger sweep over him. This was all Jack's fault. He was supposed to get ice cream, instead he had hired a canoe. And he had used Rosh's money too. The whole ten-pound note.

"What's your problem? Half of it's deposit. You'll get five pounds back!" Jack had spoken loudly and slowly, the way a condescending adult might speak to a child. Then he had added the mindless phrase that had become all too familiar to Rosh over the past few weeks: "Gosh, Rosh!" spoken with a mocking, slow shake of the head, eyes wide and an exaggerated movement of the mouth.

And then Rosh had allowed himself to be provoked into taking up the paddle and sitting behind Jack in the two-man canoe. Jack had loudly suggested that Rosh did not have the courage to venture into deep water. Now they were in deep water indeed.

He glared furiously at Jack, sitting just in front of him with his dripping paddle, raised in what seemed suspiciously like an action hero pose. The back of his cousin's head had been annoying him ever since they got into the canoe. Jack's neck currently glowed salami pink, due to a combination

4

of sunburn and physical exertion. Rosh wanted to slap him along the line where his close-cropped hair met the skin at the back of his neck.

There was something about the position of Jack's head that told Rosh exactly what kind of expression was bound to be on his cousin's face. It would be a look of annoyance. Green eyes glaring, eyebrows puckered, mouth pursed in an expression halfway between a sneer and a scowl. Never mind what kind of trouble he had got them into, Jack would not be holding up his hands and acknowledging his mistakes. No. He would be looking to place the blame elsewhere, somewhere outside of himself. Never mind that they had been swept out to sea, miles from the beach and that a mist had surrounded them, blotting out all sight of the coast and robbing them of any sense of direction. Never mind that there was some kind of monster swimming round and round their canoe. As far as Jack was concerned, Rosh thought bitterly, it was always somebody else's fault.

Then all of Rosh's anger disappeared in a moment, to be replaced by cold fear, as a pale dorsal fin rose up through the water. Rosh watched the fin as it cut through the restless surface of the sea. As it drew closer, he could make out the vast bulk of the shark beneath the water. He could see its dead eye, blank of expression, devoid of all feeling. The jaws, however, he could not see. Were there row upon row of teeth down there, or was this shark a toothless and gentle plankton eater?

It seemed they were about to find out.

2

A Lifetime

Rosh swallowed. His throat was suddenly bone dry. The shark had submerged once more and was now heading straight for them, powering through the water at a terrific pace. Rosh stared, transfixed, at the shadow in the water.

So this, he thought, is it. Rosh closed his eyes tight.

"Hey!"

He heard his cousin's voice raised in an

indignant shout, which quickly turned into a cry of alarm. The canoe lurched violently, as if an unseen giant had given it a playful flick with one enormous finger. The flimsy craft span around in the water. Rosh felt the paddle torn from his grasp as the canoe rolled over, plunging him beneath the waves.

His eyes were still tightly shut, but Rosh could sense the green darkness all around him. Instinctively he struggled to pull his legs clear of the canoe. He thrashed with his arms. A scolding voice inside his head told him he was doing the wrong thing. He should remain where he was, and calmly right the canoe. He realized the voice he was imagining sounded like Jack's. Its tone was full of cold contempt. Rosh swore heartily and his mouth filled with water. He opened his eyes. The depths spread out darkly before him. He turned his head. He was swimming downwards. There was the surface, back there, where the sunlight glimmered like a distant, starlit sky. With his lungs screaming for air, Rosh clawed his way back up.

His head broke surface and he gulped air frantically. More seawater gushed into his open mouth. His eyes stung and his chest hurt. He looked around desperately, searching for the canoe.

There it was. The pale blue fibreglass bow was suddenly right in front of him. His flailing hands grabbed at it. It seemed to hang in the water, bobbing like a fishing float. Something was wrong. The tip of the canoe was pointing skyward. Then he saw the jagged edges where the craft had been cleaved in two. The stricken canoe filled rapidly with water, then sank.

"Rosh! Over here!"

The shout came from behind him. He struggled around in the water. His clothes were sodden, heavy with water. His shirt and trousers felt like cold and clammy hands, dragging at him, pulling him down.

"Over here!"

It was Jack. He appeared to be standing on top of the water. Then the swell subsided a little and revealed a ridge of slippery rock on which his cousin stood, feet apart, hands on hips, an irritated frown on his face.

Rosh was gripped by an immense desire to get out of the water. His legs tingled in dread anticipation of powerful jaws closing on them. The back of his neck prickled and the hairs there would have stood on end had they not been plastered to his skin, soaked by the heaving waves.

He performed a wild doggy paddle, all his swimming lessons forgotten. After a few agonizingly long seconds, he reached the rocks. Jack knelt down and heaved Rosh up beside him. Rosh sprawled on the slimy surface of the stone, heaving and retching and spluttering for breath.

"That big fish," Jack said, staring out to sea, his brows knitted in an irritable frown, "that big fish, that basking shark; it's an absolute nutter!" His voice squeaked, high-pitched, a sign of his extreme annoyance. "It banged into the canoe, I think, and it must have pushed us on to these rocks. The canoe broke in half. I'll never get my deposit back now!"

Rosh raised his head and squinted at Jack, who was standing up again, legs braced, balanced on the slippery surface of the rock.

"We're stranded on a rock, in the middle of the sea, surrounded by fog, with sharks in the water and our canoe at the bottom of the ocean, and you're worrying about money," Rosh croaked, his throat still raw with salty bile. "Unbelievable! And anyway, it's *my* deposit."

But Jack was not listening. He had turned his back on the spot where the canoe had disappeared and was peering into the distance with one hand raised to shield his eyes. Rosh thought he looked like a sailor in some dodgy musical. He was going to tell him, but was suddenly seized by a fit of coughing as the last of the seawater demanded to be let out of his lungs.

The rock was hard and jagged against Rosh's knees, beneath its slippery layer of seaweed. He recalled the last time he and Jack had been side by side on a large lump of rock. Two days back. It seemed like a lifetime ago. A lifetime. Rosh was thirteen. Surely thirteen years was not enough to make up a whole lifetime. Rosh fervently hoped not.

Two days ago, the rock they had been sitting on was a gravestone. He hoped that was not going to prove prophetic. A great slab of granite, worn by the weather, covered in dry patches of lichen, grey-green and rust orange, it was one of many graves in a little churchyard they had visited, high up on a cliff overlooking the sea.

Rosh had been in a fearsome sulk. He had been scowling so much his forehead ached. History was the one subject he really could not stand. And yet here he was staying with his cousin, whose whole family seemed to love it. They watched history programmes on the telly. There were history books all over the house and there was even a history magazine, which they had delivered to the house once a week.

For the hundredth time Rosh silently cursed his parents for sending him to stay with them, and his poor grandmother for falling ill and having to be looked after. In his heart of hearts he knew his parents were right to go and stay at Grandma's so Auntie Irene could have a holiday. She lived with Grandma and took care of her all year round. She deserved a break, he could see that. And he knew, too, that he would have only been in the way in his grandmother's tiny cottage. But he cursed them all just the same, and he also cursed all the events that had conspired to lead him here, to this graveyard, where his Uncle Terry was spending hours gazing up at a crumbling church tower and wandering around graves with a notebook and a camera. The rest of them, his aunt and his cousins, all seemed quite happy about it too. That just made Rosh angrier still.

Jack had come sauntering over.

"Gosh, Rosh," he said, "not bored, are we?"

Resisting the desire to pin his cousin down and drop woodlice into his ears, Rosh turned his back and sat staring morosely out to sea. Jack sniggered but did not go away.

"My dad's been really excited about coming here, you know," he said. "You might at least pretend to be interested. He thinks it's a treat. You know how mad he is on working out our family tree. He's hoping to find the grave of one of our ancestors. And after all, they're your ancestors too. Well, half-ancestors anyway."

Rosh had bridled at that.

"They're just as much my ancestors as yours," he said. "I just don't give a stuff about them, that's all!"

On the way back in the car Jack's father had said that the sea there was wearing the cliffs away, and that last year a great chunk of land, including the far corner of the graveyard, had collapsed. The bones of people buried there hundreds of years ago had been washed up on the beach. It had made Rosh shiver.

A lifetime past. Now, Rosh and Jack were sitting on a lump of rock once more, but this time there was no family car to drive them home. If they were to get out of this situation, they would have to do it themselves.

"What's that? Over there," Jack said, pointing. Rosh continued to cough violently. "Look, shush, will you?" Jack said, wrinkling his brows. "It looks like land and it's not very far away at all. The fog must be lifting. Yes. I'm sure I'm right. That's the beach, it has to be."

What little remained of Rosh's sense of direction told him that the mainland ought to lie *behind* them, but there was no denying the grey mass of land at which Jack was now thrusting a triumphant forefinger. The landmass loomed through the thinning mist like a gigantic ghost, squatting on its haunches at the water's edge.

"It's not far. It'll only take a minute to swim across."

Rosh glanced nervously over his shoulder. Where had the shark gone? Had it just nipped around the rocks to wait for them on the other side?

Just then, a wave broke over the rocks, threatening to push them back into the water. Shark or no shark, they were going to have to take their chances and swim for it.

3

Somewhere Else

"Come on," said Jack.

"Hang on a minute," Rosh said. He began fumbling with the button of his jeans. "I'm not swimming over there in all my clothes. I nearly drowned just now." He remembered the Life Saver course he had been on back home. You had to bring along a pair of pyjamas, jump into the swimming pool while wearing them, and then practise taking them off while floating, with only the arch of your

15

back showing above the water. It was what you were supposed to do if you had to jump in and save someone's life. Rosh could not imagine it working too well in the heaving swell he had been floundering around in just now, particularly not with an unidentified shark nosing around somewhere close by.

He found that his trainers were already missing. He must have kicked them off as he struggled out of the canoe. He took off his jeans and his jacket, but left on his sodden shirt. He was already shivering with cold.

His cousin watched him, critically. Jack was dressed in shorts and a T-shirt. Although he, too, was soaked to the skin, he showed no signs of physical discomfort.

Out of habit, Rosh folded his jeans carefully and laid them on the rock. Jack lost patience.

"Come *on*," he said again and jumped into the water. There was a splash and a surprised whoop from Jack. Rosh gave a start and watched in horror as Jack suddenly rose up through the swell. He expected to see the huge head of a shark, with Jack's legs held firmly in its mighty jaws, lifting the boy, mockingly, into the air before disappearing down into the murky depths to devour him at its leisure.

Instead, Rosh saw that Jack was standing on two feet, waves lapping gently around his knees. The water was shallow on this side of the rocks.

Another wave, bigger this time, now broke over the ridge, sweeping Rosh off to join his cousin in the shallows. Rising, spluttering, from the foam, he saw the wave's backwash drag his jacket and trousers over the rocks and rapidly draw them out into deep water. Rosh sighed and turned to follow Jack, who was already wading through the shallow water in the direction of the beach.

"It must be low tide," Jack said, shouting to be heard above the sound of the waves, not bothering to turn around as he addressed his cousin. "You know, like on Holy Island, where we went yesterday, except here the sand bar is still a little bit under the water."

Jack was talking about the visit Rosh had had to endure the day before. Uncle Terry had driven them across a roadway flanked by a great expanse of ridged sand, pointing out what appeared to be a lookout post beside the road, with a ladder leading up to a sturdy platform built on stilts.

"This road'll be underwater come high tide," he had said, "that platform's for anyone who gets stuck halfway across when the waves close in."

On Holy Island, Rosh had trailed round behind his uncle, his two irritating girl cousins, Agnes and Ellie, and the equally annoying Jack, all of whom displayed huge and, to Rosh, inexplicable interest in the dreary old ruined abbey and the tedious museum that stood alongside it. To him, the Anglo-Saxons who had apparently lived there in the past were just a bunch of hairy men in smocks, of no more interest to Rosh than the hippies they resembled, who he had seen depicted in a book called *The Swinging Sixties* in the school library back home.

"It's not getting any deeper," Jack called out now. "I think we'll be able to wade all the way back to the beach!"

Rosh scowled and said nothing. The water swirled around his legs and his bare feet sank into the soft, wet sand. He wished, now, that he had not taken off his trousers. He imagined the titters and smirks of the people on the beach as he walked out of the sea, dressed in nothing but his underpants and a sopping wet shirt.

He looked up, expecting to see the beach dotted with holidaymakers, some, perhaps, already pointing in his direction and laughing. The beach, however, was empty. Not only empty, but entirely different from the sweep of golden sand backed by tussock-topped dunes where Jack had spent all Rosh's money on the stupid canoe.

Here, the seashore was scattered with boulders, worn smooth by the elements. Some were enormous, and many had large, circular holes worn into them. They resembled the gigantic bones left over from an enormous Sunday joint. The hipbones of a gargantuan lamb, perhaps, or the remnants of megalithic pork chops.

Rosh stood still. Water slopped against the back of his knees.

"Where are we?" he shouted at Jack's back. "This is a different beach. We're somewhere else, Jack!"

Jack turned his head. His brows were creased with annoyance, as if the shore was insulting him by not being the place he thought it should be. Then he shrugged and ploughed on through the swallows towards dry land. Rosh waded after him, scanning the waters on either side as he went. He was desperately trying to forget a worrying fact that had just popped into his head. He had seen it on the Did You Know? page at the back of his *Big Book of Sharks and Whales*. According to the book, the vast majority of shark attacks on humans take place in less than a metre of water.

4

The Only Way is Up

"Well, it is a beach, I suppose," Rosh said, looking around him. The weathered rocks he had noticed from out on the sandbank lay all about. Some were taller than Rosh himself. They were pock-marked and crumbled in places, smooth-surfaced in others. Some were as black as coal and others were covered with barnacles. These tiny cream-coloured shells were brick hard and razor sharp. Rosh found that out when he stubbed his toe on a barnacle-covered rock whilst wading through the last few metres of the shallows. The blood from the resulting graze, spreading in the water, had sent him scurrying on to the shingle, for fear that it would attract the shark.

"Yes, it's a beach," Rosh said again. "Sort of." Jack ignored him, looking this way and that, trying to get his bearings. "Just not *our* beach," Rosh went on.

The boys stood on a narrow strip of sand, an enormous cliff-face towering beyond it. The black rocks, fissured and craggy, were streaked by livid white stains, the droppings of the seabirds that roosted there. High above the cliffs, the boys could see a cloud of tiny speckles, black against the white of the clouds, swirling in a complex aerial interlace: birds, riding the thermals, hundreds of metres up in the air.

"Well," Jack said at last. "It looks as if the only way is up." There was an unmistakable tone of satisfaction in his voice. He was looking forward to the climb, and the knowledge that Rosh would hate it probably added to his pleasure. Or so it seemed to Rosh, who, in response, glared at the back of his cousin's head and even raised his hand to mime a slow motion swipe at the other boy's offensively pink nape.

"Come on," said Jack, pointing up at a cleft in the rock-face. "That way looks promising." He set off along the sand and began scrambling over a collection of boulders, which provided a natural, giant-sized set of steps up to where a great split in the cliff offered the chance of further footholds.

"I reckon the tide took us out towards Holy Island," Jack said. "If we get to the top of these cliffs we'll only be about ten minutes' walk from Fleming."

Rosh, following his cousin, silently contemplated Fleming. It was a small village, just a little inland from the sea. Jack and the rest of his family lived there, in a large, granite house, which had once been the home of the local squire. Curious stone sculptures, around the size of the average garden gnome, adorned the roof. The likenesses of Lord Nelson and the Duke of Wellington, two heroes from British history, stared sternly out over the gutters, flanked by a squat looking lion and a capering unicorn. Rosh would never have recognized Nelson and Wellington, of course. However, Jack, Agnes, Ellie and Uncle Terry had *all* insisted on pointing out the sculptures to him at various points throughout his first week of staying at the house. Now, despite himself, Rosh knew who they each were and had a vague, if reluctant, knowledge of their life stories.

And, despite the suffocating boredom that Rosh had endured at his cousin's home throughout the previous week, he now found himself longing for the dank hallway, its tiled floor heaped with pair upon pair of mud-encrusted walking boots, its draughty toilet with the temperamental lock and even the cold, rarely used dining room with its overpowering smell of wet dog.

With a sigh, Rosh mentally brushed away the despondent feelings that were threatening to swamp him. His pangs of longing to be somewhere else, to be *anywhere* else, would have to be ignored. He was here, on this deserted, barren strip of coast, and there was nothing he could do about it. And, to add to his misery, there was a sheer rock face to climb.

Jack had already reached the top of the pile of boulders and was clambering up the cliff itself. Rosh hurried after him, as fast as his bare feet would allow over the rocky ground. Jack was still wearing his trainers, Rosh noted enviously. Why was it that he, Rosh, was the one left looking foolish, climbing up a cliff in bare feet and no trousers, when he had done the sensible thing by discarding clothes and footwear after falling into deep water?

The climb was not as difficult as Rosh had feared. The mighty fissure up which they scrambled was criss-crossed with so many wide cracks and grooves that it formed a kind of natural ladder. Rosh's feet were becoming increasingly sore, but he was, at least, keeping up with his athletic cousin Jack.

As he climbed, Rosh obeyed the rule laid down to all reluctant mountaineers; do not look down. He could hear the sound of the waves growing steadily fainter the higher they climbed, but he avoided even the briefest of glances at the drop beneath him. He did, however, look *up* on occasion. That was when he noticed the birds.

When Rosh had first seen them, the birds had been almost out of sight, no more than distant specks in the sky. Now some elements of the flock seemed to have made a rapid descent. There were at least a dozen large gulls scything through the air, close to the cliff edge, only around ten metres above the boy's heads.

"Jack!" Rosh called. "Watch out for the birds. They're looking a bit . . ."

Jack, who was a little way ahead, looked down

at Rosh, his red bottom lip jutting out in a petulant grimace.

"What?" Jack said.

The birds were bright white, with pale grey wings, which they held straight as they sliced through the air, giving them the look of small, silent aircraft. Their heads were capped with jet-black feathers, their long, sharp-looking bills were crimson, tipped with black, and their yellow eyes glittered with unblinking malevolence.

"What did you say?" Jack called out again. He was leaning down towards Rosh, hanging on by his fingertips, seemingly unconcerned by the sickening drop down to the boulders on the beach below. A bird shot past him. Rosh heard the wind whistling over its wings as it went. Jack did not appear to notice.

"It's the birds," Rosh repeated, nervously eyeing one that was, even now, swooping past his nose. "They look a bit ... nasty," he finished, unable, under the circumstances, to think of a better way to describe the vicious-looking, living fighter planes that now filled the air all around them.

"Look out!" Jack's sudden shout had Rosh desperately scanning the sky, which seemed, for the moment, to be empty. Suddenly he felt a blast of air as something rushed past his head. At the same time he felt a searing pain in the fleshy part of his ear and heard a harsh bird call, deafeningly loud and with an unmistakable note of triumph in its tone. In the shock of the attack, Rosh let go of the rocky ledge he was grasping. He felt himself slipping down the cliff.

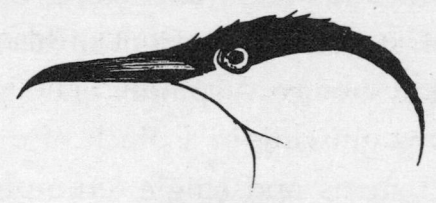

5

From the Top of the Cliff

Rosh's feet made contact, painfully, with a narrow ledge. He found himself grasping a hank of withered cliff-grass in one hand, while with the other he held on to a small lump of rock that protruded from the cliff.

His ear throbbed and he could feel a trickling wetness on his neck. Blood.

He kept his face turned towards the rock and waited, body tensed against another swooping attack. But, although the sky was filled with their raucous cries, the birds were not launching any fresh assaults. Not yet.

Rosh gritted his teeth and clung on, spread-eagled against the cliff. In front of his face there was a shallow crevice. A spindly plant, some kind of daisy, was growing in a pinch of dry soil. Its bedraggled stems and single, crumpled flower were twisted around the bones of a baby bird, which must have fallen from a nest at the top of the cliff. It seemed to regard Rosh balefully through its empty eye sockets. He gazed back.

Once again, he heard a swishing sound as a bird sliced past him, like a curved sword singing through the air.

There was a rattle of falling pebbles and then Jack's voice, close at hand.

"Yah! Yah! Yah!" Jack was shouting at the swooping gulls.

Rosh felt a mixture of relief and resentment. His cousin had come to his rescue.

"Yah! Yah!" Jack's cries, loud and haughty in tone, sounded faintly ludicrous. Rosh expected him to add, "Be off with you!" or some other old-fashioned phrase.

Jack had climbed down to within a metre or

so of where Rosh had fallen. As well as shouting, he was also flinging pebbles at the soaring birds.

"Come on," Jack said, lowering one arm. Rosh hesitated a moment, then grasped his cousin's hand. They clambered back up the rocks. As he climbed, Rosh, without realizing what he was doing, pushed one bare foot into the crevice where the dead fledgling lay. He felt the bones grind beneath his toes. A shudder ran through him.

"Sorry!" he said softly.

"Yes, well, it's lucky I was here to help," Jack said. "Those birds are absolute nutters!"

Rosh was about to snap back that he had not been talking to Jack. But he decided to say nothing. He did not want to have to explain that he had, in fact, been talking to a dead baby bird.

The sea birds were still swooping and diving around them, coming perilously close. But none made any further full-blooded attacks on the boys, who had now reached the top of the cliffs. A gentle slope, dotted with withered gorse bushes, led away from the cliff edge.

Jack sat down and blew out his cheeks.

"Phew!" he said. Rosh stood a little way back from the edge and tentatively felt his ear.

"Sit down," Jack said. "Have a rest. I reckon we'll be able to see Fleming from up on that ridge."

Rosh stayed on his feet. After falling into the sea, wading on to the beach and climbing up the cliff, his underpants were now filled up with sand and bits of gravel. He tried to shake out the debris surreptitiously, while Jack looked out to sea, watching the now distant birds.

"They must have nests with eggs in around here somewhere. That's why they attacked us," he said.

"It's summer," said Rosh, shaking his right leg. "I thought birds laid their eggs in the spring." He shook his left leg.

"Well, why else would they attack us?"

Rosh was silent for a moment.

"There's something weird about this place," he said at last. "First our canoe gets bitten in half by a shark—"

"Oh, come on, the canoe hit the rocks!" Jack tried to shout him down but Rosh carried on talking.

"First the canoe is bitten in half, then we're attacked by killer birds!"

"Oh, they're hardly killers!"

"Look at my ear! It's practically hanging off! I'm just saying," Rosh concluded, looking down at his scratched and bleeding feet, "there's something weird about this place."

"Well," said Jack, standing up, "I don't see anything strange about the Northumbrian coast. We've been living here for five years now and the weirdest thing I've come across in all that time is your haircut!"

He set off up the slope, reaching the gorse bushes in less than a minute. He stopped. Rosh, unconsciously attempting to pat down the wild jet-black tuft of hair that stood up on the crown of his head like the crest of a cockatoo, squinted up at his cousin. Jack was staring wildly about him. His features were creased in a look of confusion mixed with exasperated rage.

"What's up?" said Rosh, limping up the slope. His feet were covered in painful cuts and grazes.

"I don't understand," Jack said, "I just don't understand."

For instead of looking out over a patchwork of fields and woodland, with the roofs of Fleming village peeping through the trees, the two boys were met with a very different view.

"We're not on the mainland at all," Rosh said. "We're on an island! A tiny island! You can see right across to the other side of it from up here. I *knew* there was something not quite right about the place!"

Jack shot him a furious glance.

"Well, we can't be on one of the Farne Islands," he said quickly, making an effort to force the authority back into his voice, "we never could have drifted so far south. This must be some unknown lump of rock south-east of Holy Island."

"Just because you've never heard of it, doesn't mean it's unknown," Rosh said, mildly. He was still enjoying the fact that Jack had got things so wrong. He would have to start worrying about how they would get off the island soon, but he was making the most of this passing moment while he could. He waved an arm expansively to take in the whole island and went on, "I mean, it can't be that obscure a place. It's not just a rock, there's grass and bushes and trees. There are some grubby-looking sheep. And look, there's even a house!"

Rosh could not help a broad grin forming upon his lips. If there were people living here they must have some way of getting to and from the mainland. A jetty and a motor launch, perhaps, down on the other side of the island. There were probably boats every hour taking holidaymakers from Berwick-upon-Tweed on brief but bracing sea cruises. A bus from Berwick would have them back in Fleming by teatime.

Below them, half-hidden by a row of twisted, grey-limbed trees, the house on the island stood waiting.

6

All Men are Grass

The slopes that led down from the cliff top were covered in grass and gorse bushes, but it was by no means an easy walk. The landscape took the form of a gigantic flight of steps. After picking their way across a plateau covered by tussocks of long, straggly grass, on which the two boys were constantly tripping up, they came to a sudden drop; a low cliff of bare, broken rock. Down this they had to scramble before beginning the hike across the next stretch of dry grass.

It was hot by this time, the sun having broken through the thinning cloud soon after they had scaled the cliffs. Rosh's shirt had dried quickly, though it left his skin sticky with sea salt.

As they approached the edge of the next drop, Jack suddenly turned to Rosh with his finger pressed against his lips. They both heard the voices, coming from somewhere a little below them. Voices singing.

Although Rosh, over the past two weeks, had fallen into the habit of instantly disagreeing with everything his cousin said, on this occasion he did not ignore the unspoken call for silence. There was something strange about hearing those voices raised in song. A girl's voice, and that of two men. They were singing some kind of hymn, with great gusto, but not much tune.

Jack and Rosh looked at each other.

"What are they doing?" Rosh mouthed silently.

Jack shrugged. "Let's have a look," he whispered back. He fell to his knees and crept up to the line of bushes beyond which the ground fell away. Rosh followed him.

The two boys found themselves peering through a small gap in the sprawling thicket. The row of bushes overhung a gentle slope, which lay some three or four metres below them, covered in the usual tussocky grass.

Three figures stood on the slope. They were grouped at the side of a large hole in the ground, next to an enormous pile of newly dug earth. It was heaped up as high as the shoulders of the tallest of the three people, testament to the depth and size of the hole itself. As the sound of their voices had implied, there was a girl, around Rosh and Jack's age, a large man, who was holding a shovel in one thick-fingered hand, and a tall, white-haired older man, leaning on a silver-topped walking stick. All three were dressed in black. They finished singing and stood for a moment, heads bowed, at the side of the gaping hole. Then the old man cleared his throat.

"We are gathered here," he intoned in a clipped, upper-class accent, "to mourn the passing of Old Raw. All men, indeed all creatures, are grass. We are cut down without a thought, harvested, willy-nilly, by the Grim Reaper himself, turned into worm food and left pushing up the daisies . . ."

"Uncle Algy?" the girl interrupted. "Are you sure those are the proper words?"

"Yes, my dear," he replied solemnly. "Those are

the words of the authorized funeral service, as far as I recall them." He cleared his throat again and opened his mouth to continue his oration. Before he could speak however, the large man with the shovel blew his nose loudly on an enormous cotton handkerchief that he had extracted, with something of a struggle, from the back pocket of his denim overalls. The old man shot his companion an irritated glance.

"Really, Hobbs!" he said, crossly. "Do you have to?" He smoothed down the ends of his white moustache. Hobbs looked at the ground, shifting unhappily from foot to foot.

"I should jolly well think not," the old man said. "Now, where was I? Ah yes . . . Old Raw, who is now pushing up daisies, dearly departed, late lamented, in a word, stone dead. May he rest in peace. Amen."

"Amen," the girl repeated, loudly. She stepped forward. Peering down from his hiding place behind the gorse bushes, Rosh could see the tracks of tears, running down over her heavily-freckled cheeks. Uncle Algy, meanwhile, was making impatient gestures at Hobbs, who looked at him blankly for a while before suddenly blinking, presumably as he recalled what he was supposed to do next. The large man lumbered around to the mound of earth and, with a great deal of panting and groaning, proceeded to drag something out from behind it, something very large. He manhandled it across the grass, over to the edge of the hole. The thing was wrapped up in what appeared to be an old carpet.

"What's going on?" Rosh whispered, close to Jack's ear. "What *are* they doing?"

"Looks like some kind of weird funeral," Jack whispered back. The two boys continued to watch, fascinated.

Hobbs heaved the bulky object over the edge, letting it fall. As he did so, the carpet unwound itself, and something big tumbled out and landed with a sickening thud in the bottom of the hole. The carpet slid in after it, half covering whatever lay in the grave, obscuring it from Rosh and Jack's view.

"What was it? Did you see?" Jack asked, still speaking in a barely audible whisper. Rosh shook his head. Jack wriggled forward, craning for a clearer view into the pit.

By the graveside, the girl had begun to speak.

"Bye-bye, dear Old Raw. I know you weren't exactly what you might call all that nice, really, but we shall still miss you awfully. I don't mind that you never used to let me ride on your back, like I wanted to when I was little, or that you used to growl at me every time I went past your den, or that you used to steal my dolls and chew them into little bits. And I know you used to smell really rather awful, but I never minded that, well, not much anyway, and, yes, it was cruel the way you were always trying to bite poor Hobbs" – here the big man, who was fumbling for his handkerchief once more, nodded ruefully – "but despite all that . . ." the girl halted and screwed up her face before sobbing her concluding words, ". . . we're going to miss you!" And she burst into a fit of weeping.

She made no attempt to hold back her tears. Hobbs blew his nose again, with a sound as deep and mournful as a foghorn. Uncle Algy tut-tutted loudly.

"For goodness' sake, Bernie," he said, addressing the weeping girl, "pull yourself together! It's bad enough that old Hobbs is snivelling away like a tiny tot without *you* joining in as well. Think of who you are, blast the pair of you! Stiff upper lip! Stiff upper lip!" And he clapped his hands together making a dry sound, like a stone dropped on to a pile of autumn leaves.

Hobbs blew his nose again and the girl, Bernie, sniffed and gulped her way to silence.

"You're right, Uncle Algy," she said, when her sobbing had subsided. "We should be more like Old Raw. *He* wouldn't have got upset if it was any of *us* being buried."

While this conversation had been going on, Jack had been edging forward, a centimetre at a time. Rosh tapped him on the back, hoping to persuade his cousin to keep himself hidden. It did not seem like a good time to be asking these people for help. They were obviously in the middle of some strange and highly personal ritual. They were unlikely to look kindly on an interruption by strangers. He was going to suggest that they crept away and tried to find someone else on the island to help them.

But it was no good. Jack was clearly determined to see whatever it was that was being buried on the slope below. He ignored Rosh's tapping and leaned out still further. Rosh heard him give a gasp, then, rather too rapidly pull himself back from the brink.

"It's a *bear*!" he said, incredulously. "A whacking great dead bear! I can't believe it! Oh . . ." he added, "and I think they've seen us."

"Hey! You!" Uncle Algy's voice barked out. His tone was cold and commanding. "Show yourselves, both of you! We know you're there!"

7

Down the Gully

"OK, OK! We're coming down!" Jack called out straight away.

"What are you doing?" Rosh grabbed his cousin by the shoulders. The two boys were on their knees now, facing one another.

Jack shrugged. "We might as well go down there. They've seen us. Besides, we need to ask someone how we get back to the mainland."

"Yes, but not them!" Rosh was aghast. "They're weird!"

"You don't know that," said Jack.

"They were having a *funeral* for a dead *bear*!" Rosh said, giving Jack's shoulders a shake. "I say we just run away," he went on. "There must be someone else on the island that could help!"

"We're waiting," Uncle Algy's voice broke in, harshly. "You don't want me to have to send Hobbs up to get you, do you?"

"Just coming!" Jack called out. He pulled away from Rosh's grasp and stood up.

"It's all very well for you," Rosh said to Jack, his voice a petulant mumble, "but I'm not wearing any trousers, remember?"

Jack looked down at Rosh and sniggered unkindly.

"Gosh, Rosh," he said, "you do look a bit of a sight." Then he set off along the ridge to where a gap in the gorse bushes offered a route down to the lower ground. He did not glance behind him to see if Rosh was following.

Rosh remained where he was for a moment, squatting on his haunches in the shadow of the gorse bushes.

"There's a second boy up there!" Uncle Algy boomed. "Come on, no slinking away, you're both in this together!"

Rosh sighed. He pulled his bedraggled shirt over his head, having decided that it would be better to be shirtless than trouserless. He knotted the shirt around his waist and stood up.

Looking down at his legs, Rosh quickly changed his mind about the shirt around the waist. He now looked as if he was wearing a skirt. He was struggling to untie the arms when Uncle Algy barked out, "You, boy! Down here! Now!" Rosh jumped. There was such an air of command to the old man's voice that Rosh found himself hurrying after Jack. He kept his head down, painfully aware that three pairs of curious eyes were following him as he limped along the ridge and then scrambled down the gully of broken rock.

Rosh joined Jack, and they stood in front of Uncle Algy. Hobbs, shovel in hand, had begun the laborious task of refilling Old Raw's vast grave. Bernie was standing next to the old man, regarding the two boys with a broad grin upon her freckled face. She seemed to have recovered her spirits very quickly after her graveside tears. Rosh caught her eye for a second, and, though her smile seemed to show friendly rather than malicious intent, he nevertheless looked quickly away.

Uncle Algy towered above them, tall, forbidding and smelling strongly of mothballs. He looked down. His hooded eyes, which glittered coldly behind a pair of half-moon spectacles, were set in a deeply-lined and weather-beaten face. Long and thin, with a haughty nose, Uncle Algy's features reminded Rosh of a picture of the unwrapped, mummified remains of Ramses the Great in a book he had been forced to use for a History project at school.

The old man regarded them in silence for a moment, thoughtfully stroking his moustache.

"Well, I never," he said at last, "if it isn't the Young Robinson Crusoe. He's even got his very own Boy Friday, too!"

Rosh scowled, regretting more than ever the rash decision to wear his shirt around his waist. As far as his facial features and general build were concerned, Rosh resembled his English father far more than he did his Sri Lankan mother. But although his skin was lighter than his mother's rich, burnt umber complexion, he was definitely several shades darker than his pale skinned, pink-necked cousin. And now here he was, bare-chested and wearing what clearly looked, to the old man, like some kind of native's loincloth. And so Uncle Algy had labelled Jack Robinson Crusoe, the white-skinned castaway, and Rosh Friday, the dark-skinned, so-called savage that Crusoe took as his unpaid servant.

He felt a rush of indignation. He was no-one's servant, least of all Jack's. However, there was something in the old man's demeanour that stopped Rosh from speaking his mind. Something of the look in those glittering eyes made him think of the gulls that had attacked them when they were climbing the cliffs. Besides, over the years, he had heard one or two old people muttering much worse things about his skin colour, back home on the streets of London. He blew a breath of air out through his nose in an angry sigh, and left it at that. Algernon did not appear to notice.

Jack stepped forward and cleared his throat.

"I'm Jack," he said pompously. "And this is my cousin, Rosh."

It was Bernie who responded.

"My real name's Bernice, but everyone calls me Bernie," said Bernie. "And this is Uncle Algy. I mean Sir Algernon. What happened to your ear?" Bernie went on brightly. She leaned towards Rosh and reached out as if to take hold of his wounded ear. Rosh backed away in alarm. Bernie shrugged and dropped her arm.

"My, my, that *does* look nasty!" Sir Algernon said, happily.

"A bird bit it," Rosh said. He stared frostily at the old man.

"Ah yes," said Sir Algernon, "you've had a run in with a common tern by the looks of it. You'd recognize the cry, I dare say, a short sharp 'kit kikiki' or an emphatic 'KEEY-yah!' They're particularly vicious on this island of ours. Mind you, I can hardly blame them. We do eat rather a lot of their eggs. Not to mention their chicks. Delicious boiled with dumplings."

The old man licked his pale lips and squinted coldly from behind his half-moon spectacles.

8

Welcome to Blood Willow Hall

Jack was chatting away to the old man in a loud, clear voice, the voice he always used when speaking to adults. He let out a peel of laughter at something Sir Algernon had said. Rosh cringed. The laugh sounded so false.

They left Hobbs still filling in Old Raw's grave and set off along a dry and sandy track winding down towards the house. It was the same house Rosh had first seen from the cliff-top.

Rosh was walking several paces behind his cousin and Sir Algernon. Jack had told the old man all about their predicament, eagerly explaining how the tide had swept them out to be lost in the sea mist and earnestly admitting that they had been very foolish indeed to take the canoe so far from the shore.

"There was a shark in the sea," Rosh mumbled, his only contribution to the conversation. At this, Sir Algernon pricked up his ears.

"Really?" he said. "How fascinating! I do hope it was a Great White. I've been getting Hobbs to throw the odd sheep carcass into the sea, out by the reef, ever since I heard that they'd seen one off the Cornish coast! It would be nice to think we've tempted such a noble killer of the deep to visit our little island. I have a great love of the big carnivores, you know," he added, by way of explanation. "I've been trying to build up a menagerie of meat-eaters, here on the island. It's rather depleted now that Old Raw's snuffed it, of course."

Sir Algernon then suggested that they join him back at a place he described as "The Hall". Jack asked if they could use the telephone to tell his parents what had happened, but the old man just laughed, and said "The Hall" did not contain anything so new-fangled as a telephone.

Bernie fell in beside Rosh as he limped along the track. He was wearing his shirt in the conventional manner again and was horribly aware of his naked legs. The skin on his face prickled with embarrassment and he kept his head down, hoping she would catch up with Jack and her uncle. But she made no attempt to speed up.

"I'm sure we can find you a pair of trousers back at the Hall," Bernie said pleasantly. "It can't be very nice going about in just a shirt and a pair of trunks. Those *are* trunks, aren't they?" Bernie shot an inquisitive glance at Rosh's legs.

"Yes!" Rosh growled, tugging his shirt down as far as it would stretch.

"Well, I don't care, really," Bernie went on, "I don't think it matters at all what people wear. I'm afraid Uncle Algy is awfully stuffy about things like that. That's why we're all dressed in black. Because of Old Raw's funeral." She slapped the flapping folds of her dress, a shapeless garment made of heavy, coarse fabric that reached down to the ground and raised a trail of dust as it dragged along the path behind her.

"Hobbs made this for me," she went on. "It's pretty ghastly, isn't it? I don't care though. I only wish he hadn't used such thick cloth! It's all very well in the winter because, believe you me, it can get pretty chilly round here, but on a summer day like this one . . . Phew! I'm sweating like a porker!"

She grabbed a hank of her thick red hair, which she was wearing in bunches bound with manila-coloured elastic bands, and dabbed at her forehead with it.

"Like a porker!" she repeated. "I say, your cousin's rather nice, isn't he?" she continued, without a break.

Rosh shot her what he hoped she would realize was a pitying look.

"There's no accounting for taste," he murmured.

"You're nice too, of course," said Bernie. "I'm sure we'll be great friends, the three of us! Wow, it'll be great to have some proper chums for once. I never get to meet anyone nice." Rosh gave her another discouraging frown, which she did not appear to notice. But she did, at least, change the subject.

Pointing up at the house, Bernie said, "Look, we're nearly there!"

Rosh took his eyes off the path for the first time and looked up. The path had taken them around the row of trees that screened the house. Their leaves gave out a dry hissing sound as the wind rippled through them. The shadows of their swaying boughs stretched across a wide expanse of closely cropped grass and on to the walls of the house itself, as if the fingers of a giant hand were feeling at the windows, seeking a way in.

Rosh shivered.

"Come on," said Bernie, "let's find you those trousers."

She took hold of Rosh by the upper arm and hurried after her uncle and Jack, who had already climbed the stone steps that led to the front door and disappeared inside. Rosh allowed himself to be led. The house towered above them, four storeys tall. A glass dome rose from the centre of the building, the sun glinting on its grimy window-panes, some of which were cracked or broken.

Two carved stone columns were set one on either side of the high doorway. The carvings on them had been almost completely worn away by years of wind and rain. Here and there it was possible to make out the remnants of figures, their limbs contorted in wild postures, their features dissolved away into blank, eyeless masks.

The door itself lay half open. A coat of arms had been carved into the wood; a shield, bearing the worn image of a twisted serpent, its huge jaws clamped around the torso of a struggling human figure, whether man, woman or child it was impossible to tell. A border set with circular roundels surrounded this gruesome device. Seeing it, Rosh remembered Uncle Terry showing him a framed imitation parchment on which all the coats of arms of the various branches of their family had been painted. He had barely glanced at the tiny shields. He felt a twinge of regret at how rude he had been. He could not believe how much he would give to be back at Uncle Terry's house right now.

Rosh shivered again as they passed through the door and into the darkened entrance hall.

"Welcome to Blood Willow Hall," said a harsh voice, close to his ear.

9

Nasty

Rosh started, violently. Sir Algernon was standing in the shadows just inside the doorway. It was he that had spoken. The old man laughed, a wheezing shudder of mirth lifting his shoulders up and down. Behind his spectacles there was a cold, predatory gleam in his eyes.

He stepped out of the shadows into the half-light of the entrance hall. Jack was still with him, wearing a baffled smile, as if he did not know whether to join their host in laughing at the way he had made Rosh jump, or not.

"I expect you boys would like some tea," Sir Algernon said. His tone was suddenly light and pleasant once more. "Come this way."

There were two stairways ascending from the entrance hall, one to the right and one to the left. Rosh followed Jack and Algernon to the right. Bernie ran up the other stairway, her feet clattering on the uncarpeted steps.

"I'll just have a look for those trousers," she called over her shoulder. "I'm sure Hobbs was experimenting with trouser-making during the winter. He won't mind lending you one of the pairs that didn't quite work. Or I don't think he'll mind, I haven't actually asked him yet, of course, but . . ." Her voice faded away as she disappeared out of sight and the sound of her running footsteps dwindled into silence.

Jack waited for Rosh to catch up. Algernon was moving slowly up the stairs with one hand resting lightly on the banister.

"This place is fantastic," Jack whispered, excitedly. "Sir Algernon must be really rich! Look at that banister, it'd be brilliant to slide down."

"Yeah, until you hit one of those," Rosh said, nodding towards a carved griffin, its sharp beak raised as if to deliberately impale anyone light-spirited enough to attempt to use the banister as anything other than an oversized handrail. The griffin was one of a menagerie of carved beasts that reared up every few metres, whenever the stairs met a turn or a landing.

"If you ask me," Rosh went on, dropping his voice so that Algernon would not overhear, "the whole place is a bit of a dump. It's so old! And there's dust everywhere, and it's all broken. Look at that statue, for instance."

"It's *meant* to be like that, you idiot," Jack said. "Look, its head's down there, on the base."

Rosh squinted at the headless stone figure, which stood in the small, gloomy landing at the top of the first flight of steps. He saw that Jack was right. It was a sculpture of a decapitated man, his head lying at his feet. Someone had painted streams of gloss red, running down from his neck. It was pretty unconvincing blood but it still gave Rosh a chill.

"Well, that's just nasty," Rosh said. "It's giving me the creeps. The sooner we're out of here, the better. Stop being so friendly with these people,

Jack! Didn't you ever do stranger/danger stuff at school? Let's just ask them to get us a boat or whatever so we can get back to the mainland."

"Come along, you two," Sir Algernon called out. He was some way ahead of them by now, close to the top of the stairs. "No dilly-dallying back there!"

"There's nothing to worry about," Jack said to Rosh, "he's a 'Sir,' for goodness' sake! He must be rolling in money. I expect he's got his own yacht. I bet he'll take us off the island as soon as he's had his afternoon tea. Just coming, Sir Algernon!" he called, hurrying up the stairs.

Rosh followed without quickening his pace. Jack was far too eager to please this scary old man, Rosh thought. He decided that he, at least, was not going to hurry. Besides, his feet were still hurting.

He plodded upstairs. The polished wooden steps were cool and smooth beneath his damaged soles. As he climbed, he cast a disinterested eye over the paintings that hung, three deep, on the stairwell wall.

One glowering landscape caught his attention. He paused for a moment and gazed at it. There was something in the lie of the land that looked familiar. Rosh frowned, then gave a nod as he recognized the skyline he had seen after climbing up the cliff. The painting depicted a scene on the island itself. It was a very dark and dreary picture, thickly varnished, in a dusty frame. Rosh frowned as he took in the colour scheme, which looked as though the artist had used a selection of different gravies instead of paint. The smeary, painted sky was heavy with brown storm clouds; the gorse bushes on the skyline were bent over, suggesting that a strong gust of wind was blowing through them. In the shadowy foreground, there was a tree-lined field.

Rosh leaned forward, peering through the glassy surface of the painting. It was like looking into a murky pond and trying to see down to the bottom. Rosh blinked and looked closer at the lower portion of the canvas. The landscape was inhabited. There were people on the field, dressed in breeches, long socks and three-cornered hats. Even Rosh, with his total lack of interest in history, could tell that their costumes dated from a period several hundred years in the past. But what were they doing? Some were standing round, seemingly inactive. One man appeared to be running with one arm held high above his head. He was holding something in his hand, shaping to throw it, hard. All eyes were turned to the direction in which the throw was aimed. Rosh followed the collective gaze of the little painted men. He saw a hunched figure, cowering in the left-hand corner of the painting. He was holding up a stick or club of some kind, with which, it seemed, he hoped to fend off the missile that was about to strike him. His face was a mask of terror. Rosh noted, with a shock, that his ankle was clapped in an iron cuff, chained to a wooden stake, which was driven into the ground a metre or so behind him.

Rosh was about to turn away from the painting in disgust. Whatever local pastime it was commemorating, it looked like something he would rather not know about. Then he spotted a figure in the bottom corner. It was a man; clearly more expensively dressed than the others in the painting. He was standing in the shade of a stunted willow tree, one hand resting on the gilded hilt of an elegant sword. The artist had painted him with his head turned so that he looked out at the viewer. There was a distinctly unpleasant smile upon his lips. And there was something unsettlingly familiar about his glittering eyes.

10

Crossed Like Swords

By the time Rosh reached the top of the stairs, Algernon and Jack were disappearing down a dingy corridor. He limped after them.

Sir Algernon led the way to a gloomy and cluttered little room, the walls of which were decorated with an array of moth-eaten animal heads, mounted on wooden shields, and what looked like an assortment of equipment for use in some obscure sport.

"Here we are, chaps," said Algernon, "the trophy room! Ideal place for a spot of tiffin, I'd say." He beamed at the two boys, who stared back at him, blankly.

"Tea," he explained. "Time for tea!"

The old man walked back towards the door to where a dusty-looking, silken cord hung down from a fitting in the ceiling. He tugged at it with an impatient jerk of the hand. There was the sound of bells jangling in distant parts of the house.

After waiting for no more than a couple of seconds, Sir Algernon made a dry tutting sound with his tongue, and then moved out into the corridor. He looked both ways, his features creased in a frown of annoyance.

"Hobbs!" he bellowed, "Hobbs! Drat the man, where is he? There's two boys and an old 'un here, all dying of thirst!"

"Isn't he burying your . . . your pet?" asked Jack.

"That's no excuse!" fumed Sir Algernon, pacing up and down the corridor. "He should have finished that by now! The man's an idler to the bone! To the bone, I say! I venture I shall find him in one of the basement rooms, trying his hand at some fancy double-stitching technique he's read about in a back copy of *The Home Tailor* he's found washed up on the shore! If so, I shall make him jump, believe you me. Wait here, boys. I shall return with Hobbs carrying a tray laden with tea things, or, failing that, *I* shall be carrying a tray laden with Hobbs' head!" And the old man set off along the corridor at a brisk pace, angrily striking the skirting board with his cane as he went.

"Poor old Hobbs," said Jack, when Sir Algernon was out of hearing range. "Sounds like he's for it."

Rosh was in no mood to be sympathetic, however.

"If that big fool chooses to stay on this island," he said, belligerently, "working for some mental old man, then that's his lookout. But I don't think we should hang about. You see what Sir Algernon's like when he loses his temper? Let's get out of here, Jack."

But Jack was not listening.

"Fascinating house, this," he said. He was studying the contents of the trophy room with every sign of avid interest. "This timber-wolf was killed in 1879 by Sir Havelock Blood Willow," he said, squinting at the tarnished bronze plaque below one sorry-looking stuffed relic. "Must have been one of Algernon's ancestors."

"What, the wolf or Sir Havelock?" Rosh said. "Come on. Let's go."

"Look at these things," said Jack, ignoring Rosh and examining two curved clubs, "what on earth are *they* for? They look like old-fashioned cricket bats!" Long-handled and made from wood, they hung, crossed like swords, upon the wall beneath the wolf's head, which, with its glass eyes cloudy with dust, was staring glumly into the middle distance.

"Talking of Algernon's relatives," Rosh said, "I think I saw a picture of one of them on the stairs. He was watching some nasty-looking local custom. By the look on his face he seemed to be enjoying it, too. Look, it's obvious these people liked being cruel to animals, to people, to whatever. And by the way Sir Algy's gone after Hobbs, it looks like it runs in the family. So I think we should leg it, *now*, before he comes back with the tea or the tiffany or whatever it was he called it. There must be someone else on this island who can get us back across the water."

Jack, engrossed in studying the various artefacts displayed in the trophy room, waved a dismissive hand at his cousin.

"You go if you like. I mean, if you're frightened, Rosh . . ."

Rosh felt a flash of anger burn through him, but

he was determined not to let Jack get to him that way again. If he had ignored Jack's taunting and refused to get into the canoe in the first place, then they would never have ended up here at all. Rosh turned on his heel and walked out. Behind him, Jack was still talking.

"There was something really familiar about that coat of arms on the front door. I wish I could remember where I've seen it before," he said. Rosh did not stop to listen. Leaving the room, he turned into the corridor and walked blindly, breathing noisily through his nose as he padded over the heavily-worn carpet, letting his anger cool.

"Fine. You stay," he muttered under his breath, "but I'm off. I'm not ending up with my head stuck up on the wall."

He turned into an open doorway and found himself on a dark landing. There was a wrought-iron spiral staircase in front of him.

Rosh heard a clang and clatter above him. Someone had stepped on to the iron stairs. He looked up. A shadow moved.

"Who's that?" said Rosh, suddenly afraid. His voice was quiet in the silence of the darkened stairwell.

11

Crumbling Volumes

"Oh, it's you Rosh! Here're some trousers!" He recognized Bernie's voice instantly, but it made him jump just the same. A bundle of fabric came hurtling down the tube-like space in the centre of the spiral stairs and flumped on to the bare boards at Rosh's feet, raising a cloud of dust as it landed.

"Hobbs doesn't mind, honest!" Bernie called out from above. "I've told him you're my friend. I suppose he might seem a bit odd when you first meet him, but he's very nice, really. He promised my mum and dad he'd look after me, you know, just before they had their accident. I'll just see if I can find you some shoes and socks." There was a squeak of shoe leather on metal and then the patter of footsteps receding quickly into silence. Rosh stood for a moment, looking up through the curving ironwork staircase, into the thick darkness of the floor above. Bernie was either a brazen liar or the history of this household was even stranger than it appeared. And considering the appearance of Blood Willow Hall and its inhabitants, that would make it very strange indeed.

If she were really telling the truth, then that would explain why Hobbs put up with working for such a short-tempered employer. He stayed to keep Bernie from harm. Rosh wondered whether the big man's protection would be extended to Jack and himself. Hobbs' grimfaced silence and drooping, melancholy eyes hardly inspired confidence.

Rosh bent down and picked up the bundle that Bernie had thrown him.

"Well," Rosh said to himself, holding the garment out at arm's length to examine it, "it *is* a pair of trousers, I suppose."

The trousers were made of thick, dark crimson velvet. It was the sort of cloth the stage curtains in a theatre might be made of. The velvet pile was worn away in places. It put Rosh in mind of a short-haired animal suffering from a nasty skin disease. The seams had been sewn together with broad stitches using thick, white twine.

He pulled on the trousers and found them ridiculously large. Luckily, there was a belt, strung around the waist through hoops of string that had been sewn on to the waistband. He tightened the belt to its final notch then knelt down to roll up the trailing trouser legs. But no matter how ludicrous he looked, Rosh was still greatly relieved to be fully dressed again. With a stab of guilt, he realized that he had not even said thanks.

Another realization was dawning on Rosh. He did not know how to get outside. He was lost in Blood Willow Hall.

Rosh peered up at the spiral stairs. Bernie was up there somewhere. If he could find her she could tell him how to get out.

He climbed the stairs. The unfamiliar folds of the velvet curtain trousers billowed around his legs. The wrought-iron stairs rang out a dull and muffled chime with every step he took.

He reached another dingy landing. Was that noise Bernie, moving around on the floor above? He continued up the twisting stairway, the ironwork steps pressed painfully beneath his sore feet.

He reached the top of the iron staircase. Another gloomy landing. Two doors led off it. They were both closed. Again, Rosh thought he heard Bernie's distant footsteps. The sound came from behind the door to his right. He opened it.

Rosh was expecting another dark corridor, but instead, as he pulled open the door, the landing was flooded with light. Blinking, he shuffled out on to a railed walkway, about half a metre wide. The walkway ran around the inside wall of a large, octagonal gallery, roofed over with a domed canopy of glass panes. Some of them were cracked or broken and all of them were streaked with dirt. This, then, was the dome that Rosh had noticed from outside, rising up from the centre of the house. All the other rooms, the whole of Blood Willow Hall, he realized, must be built around this huge, central space.

And this space housed a vast library of old books. Shelves filled with crumbling leather-bound volumes covered the walls, from the ground floor up to where he now stood. A second walkway ran around the dome, level with the floor below, and provided access to yet more rows of books, while, on the ground floor, an arrangement of free standing bookcases enclosed a large oak table on which a couple of hefty tomes lay open. On all three levels, there were four doors, one above the other. Rosh supposed there would be three other spiral staircases behind the other doors too, providing access to the library from all parts of the house.

Rosh stood at the iron railing, feeling the metal cold under his palms. He peered down at the floor below. There were two sets of double doors at opposite ends of the library. One or other of them must lead back to the entrance hall. All he had to do was to take one of the staircases down to enter the library at ground level.

Now that he had got his bearings, Rosh decided he didn't need Bernie's help to find his way out. He had no intention of waiting around for her to find him some shoes, despite his throbbing feet. As soon as he got out and found a farm or a village, preferably a fishing village where they could borrow a boat to get them to the mainland, he would come back for Jack and they would be on their way.

Now that his anger had cooled, Rosh was finding it difficult not to think about Jack. He had walked out and left him. It was true, Jack annoyed him. But he was his cousin: safe, familiar, annoying Jack. Rosh wondered if he had made a mistake heading off alone.

About halfway round the upper walkway, there was a short flight of steps, squeezed into a narrow space between two bookshelves. These steps led up to the lowest of the glass panes of the dome itself. He sat down on the bottom step. Indecision stopped him in his tracks. Maybe he should go back for Jack *now*? He could not decide what to do.

A still, dark shape caught his eye. Something was perched on the stair rail above him, up by the glass on the inside of the dome. Rosh gazed up at it. It was a large bird with greasy black feathers, sitting, hunched up and with its head sunk down between its shoulders. About a metre tall from claws to head, it remained totally motionless. There was a forlorn, rather dusty look about it, as though it had been sitting there for a very long time.

"It must be stuffed," Rosh muttered to himself. "It looks like a vulture. A stuffed vulture. I wonder why they put it up there?"

At the back of his mind Rosh was aware that he was deliberately delaying the decision about whether to leave now or go back for Jack. If he did return, it would be like admitting he had been wrong to storm off in the first place. He chose to study the vulture for a while instead.

The eyes of the stuffed bird were particularly realistic. They were small and beady and imbued with glowering malice. But what were they made of? Glass? Some kind of bead? Rosh took another step up. How was that sparkle achieved? He climbed the remaining stairs and stood beside the vulture. He leant forward, peering into its face.

The pink skin on the bird's naked head was puckered and slimy looking. The feathers were dishevelled, giving the creature a ragged, unkempt appearance. The eyes, however, were remarkably realistic. They even seemed to blink.

"Well," Rosh said to the stuffed bird, "you're an ugly-looking devil, aren't you?"

The vulture suddenly reared up, its neck unfurling like a snake about to strike, its wings flapping, wafting out a terrible stink of rotten meat. A dry, hissing rattle sounded in the creature's throat.

Rosh uttered a cry of horror and surprise. He

threw himself backwards. Too late, he realized that he had fallen against the cracked window-pane. The glass shattered about his shoulders. He felt himself plummeting backwards into thin air.

12

Teasing Henry

The world seemed to move in slow motion. Rosh felt himself perform an involuntary back-flip and saw his legs passing over his head in a shower of broken glass. He landed heavily, rolling on his back.

Having expected to be plunging, with a dying scream, to the ground below, it was a great relief for Rosh to find himself lying on a narrow ledge. The ledge ran around the outside at the base of the dome. A stone balustrade surrounded it.

Placing his hands on the rough, moss-covered stone, Rosh pulled himself to his feet and shook his voluminous trousers. Shards of glass tinkled on to the stone floor. The thickness of the material had saved Rosh from serious injury. A few tiny slivers of glass were still stuck into the crimson velvet, but Rosh himself remained unharmed.

He peered cautiously back through the broken glass panel. What had happened to the vulture? He soon found out. With a blood-curdling squawk, and another blast of fetid air generated by its beating wings, the vast and cumbersome bird suddenly launched itself out through the now empty glass frame. Advancing rapidly along the ledge, it lunged at Rosh with its cruelly curved beak, uttering a furious guttural hissing from somewhere deep in its throat.

Rosh let out a moan of despair. His only option was to vault the balcony and try to escape across the steeply sloping roof. Trying to ignore the very real danger that he would slip over, slide down the roof and be pitched out over the guttering and on into empty space, Rosh leapt the barrier. With a hideous screech, the vulture came after him, spreading its wings and heaving its bulky frame into cumbersome flight.

Rosh, skittering across the roof tiles, felt a shadow fall over him. The vulture hung, seemingly suspended in the air above his head. Rosh found himself staring into the beady eyes that, only a few moments before, he had been admiring as a fine example of a taxidermist's skill. There was no pity in those inhuman eyes. With a contemptuous cackle, the vulture dived.

Rosh threw himself forward to avoid the questing talons of the ferocious bird. He hit the roof hard and felt the tiles crack beneath his knees. Then he was slipping, balance gone, with no chance of a handhold anywhere.

His bare feet hit the gutter. It came away under his weight. With a horrified cry, Rosh slid over the roof's edge, along with an avalanche of broken tiles. Yelling wordlessly, in the grip of total panic, he flailed out at the only possible handhold he could see. His desperate fingers clamped themselves around a short length of pipe that protruded from the brickwork, just below where the guttering had been.

Rosh hung from the pipe. Without looking down, he probed the air with his feet. No footholds. Just a sheer brick wall on one side, the empty sky on the other, and a long drop below.

He swallowed. The pipe had been painted green once, long ago. A few dry green flakes crumbled off and drifted down into his eyes.

There was a sudden disturbance in the air and the sun was blotted out by a shadow. The vulture swept down from the roof and perched on the pipe. Its talons grasped the metal tube on either side of Rosh's whitening knuckles.

The boy hung his head, his eyes firmly closed. The thought of the great bird's curved beak slashing at his face flashed through his mind. He would not even be able to cover his eyes.

A voice was calling from somewhere below his feet. It was Bernie.

"Rosh! Rosh, what are you doing?"

Rosh heard her as if from a great distance. A dreamlike sense of calm had descended on him as he hung from the pipe with the vulture squatting above him. With a detached sense of curiosity, he noted the pain in both his arms and the gradual loosening of his grip on the pipe.

"Rosh!" Bernie's voice floated up to him. "Come down from there. I've got you some shoes and socks."

Rosh noticed his chest heaving and heard the wheezy giggle that escaped his own lips. Perhaps, minutes from death, he was just imagining Bernie's voice. How could she be chatting to him about shoes and socks when he was about to fall to his doom?

The vulture shifted its claws on the pipe. It uttered an impatient-sounding squawk. Rosh felt the creature lower its beak to the fingers of his left hand and begin to prise them from the pipe. Rosh pulled his hand away. He heard himself let out a low moan. The fingers on his right hand lost their grip. He was falling.

The impact came all too quickly. Almost immediately, in fact. His legs buckled under him and his body slammed into cold, hard stone. Rosh gasped.

He was winded. Winded but not dead. Winded, but not even injured. He rolled over on to his back and slowly opened his eyes.

Sir Algernon was standing over him, peering down through his half-moon spectacles, twirling one end of his silver moustache between finger and thumb. The vulture let out an angry screech and beat its wings disconsolately. Sir Algernon frowned.

"Oh dear," he said to Rosh, "I hope you haven't been teasing Henry."

13

Fresh Meat

Bernie was standing next to her uncle, holding, in one hand, a pair of ancient looking sea-boots and, in the other, two grey woollen socks. The socks waved like medieval pennants in the breeze. She grinned and held the footwear out towards Rosh.

Behind her was a set of French windows, opening out on to the wide, stone balcony on to which Rosh had fallen. After crashing through the dome and sliding off the roof beneath it he had been seconds from plunging down the front face of the building. But when he had grabbed hold of the pipe that broke his fall, this balcony could only have been a metre or so beneath his feet. If he had glanced down he would have known that. But he had not wanted to look down.

Algernon stepped over Rosh and whistled breathily between his teeth. There was a clatter of claws and a flapping of wings. The vulture landed clumsily on the stone balustrade.

"Hello, Henry," Sir Algernon said. "Who's a handsome feller, then?"

Rosh rose groggily to his feet. Sir Algernon patted the odious Henry on the top of his featherless head.

"I think Henry was hoping you'd miss the balcony and fall all the way to the ground." Sir Algernon chuckled.

"It's not funny!" Rosh said, suddenly angry. "Your pet bird just tried to eat me!"

"Eat you? Good heavens, no!" said Algernon. "Henry wasn't trying to *eat* you. He'd never eat live flesh. He was just trying to kill you. Then he would have left you for a day or two, just until you started to turn mouldy, and *then* he would have eaten you. You can't abide fresh meat, can you, Henry?"

"Oh well, that's all right then!" Rosh said. "Henry only wanted to kill me. That's great, that's fine, that is!"

"There you are, Henry, old lad," Sir Algernon said to the hulking great bird, "young Rosh doesn't mind a bit. He just said so himself."

Again, the old man patted the vulture's head. Henry hunched his shoulders sulkily, but nevertheless seemed prepared to tolerate Sir Algernon's affections.

Rosh however, was speechless. All the fear that he had felt drain away into hopeless resignation when he hung from the pipe, waiting for what he thought would be an agonizing end, now boiled over into fury, filling him up with rage. He felt liable to explode.

Rosh pushed past Bernie, snatching the socks and boots from her as he went. He stormed through the room, which appeared to be some kind of study, and out on to a landing. There he saw Jack, standing near the top of a staircase.

"Oh, there you are, Rosh," Jack said, "I thought I heard voices."

"Come on," said Rosh, grabbing his cousin firmly by the wrist, "we're leaving. Now!"

He marched down the stairs, almost dragging Jack

behind him and ignoring all his shouts of protest and annoyance. Other voices called over his cousin's constant yelling. Bernie seemed to shout some kind of warning. Sir Algernon also raised his voice, but his tone was smug and mocking.

Rosh was listening to none of them. The two boys reached the hallway, crossed to the front door and were halfway down the dusty pathway that led away from the house before Jack managed to pull his hand free. He turned on his cousin.

Jack's face and neck were bright pink. He was now every bit as angry as Rosh was. Without a word, he flew at him with flailing fists. Rosh stretched out both palms. Jack ran into them. His fists whirled past Rosh's nose but his arms were too short to make any contact. Rosh grabbed him by the shoulders and held him still.

Panting with exertion, tongue protruding from his mouth, Jack now tried to launch a few savage kicks at Rosh. But Rosh skipped backwards, pulling Jack off balance, and then swept his feet from under him in one swift lunge of his own right leg. Jack crashed to the ground, flat on his back, raising a cloud of dust. Rosh was upon him in an instant, pinning his arms to the ground before Jack could move.

From the onset of the fight, Rosh's anger had suddenly deserted him. He felt only astonishment at Jack's wild attack. He was perturbed too, by its complete ineffectiveness. His surprise and embarrassment grew tenfold however when he realized that furious tears were spurting from his cousin's eyes and rolling down his burning cheeks.

Rosh released Jack's arms and jumped to his feet. He walked a few paces away and stood, turned to one side, surreptitiously watching the other boy from the corner of his eye. Then, to cover his confusion, he knelt down and quickly put on the itchy woollen socks and cracked leather boots that Bernie had given him, a gift he had, once again, failed to thank her for.

Jack dragged himself up on to his elbows and clawed at his streaming eyes. He did not try to conceal his tears. The heaving and shuddering of his chest eased after a few minutes and he turned a glowering, puffy-eyed gaze on Rosh before he spoke.

"I wish you'd never come to stay," he said. The tremor of a fading sob half choked his words. "I wish I'd never had anything to do with you! I wish I wasn't even your cousin!"

Rosh looked at Jack. He felt bewildered. Where was the sneering, pink-necked canoeist and mountaineer now? Where was the boy that had been making Rosh's life a misery for the past two weeks? Jack was a snivelling wreck.

"You've totally ruined our summer holiday!" Jack went on, scrambling to his feet and dusting himself down. He seemed to be warming to his theme. "You get foisted on us for three whole weeks," he continued, "and then you have the nerve to mope about the house like a wet weekend, whinging and complaining about everything we do!"

Rosh looked at the ground. Was that really how he had behaved?

"And then," Jack went on, "you get us stranded on some island or other, and you drag me out of a very interesting old house and you pull me down the stairs and virtually break my wrist!"

Rosh shook his head. Now Jack had gone too far.

"You're unbelievable, you are!" he said. "So it's my fault we're on this island, is it? Well that's news to me."

By now, the boys were stomping along the path together, neither paying much attention to where they were heading. The dust from the path billowed up from their stamping feet like smoke. They marched on in silence, darting each other the occasional angry glare. It was a while before it occurred to Rosh that Jack was now, it seemed, following his original suggestion to look for help elsewhere. For Jack to be doing something, however reluctantly, that someone else had suggested was definitely a first.

Away to their right, a steep-sided hill rose up. Its flattened summit was crowned with a wide circle of gnarled and twisted trees. A few bony sheep were rooting around in the tall, tough-looking grass on the hillside. The evening sun was sinking down behind the brow of the hill and the long shadow it cast seemed to stretch out, like a giant hand, towards the grim outline of Blood Willow Hall, by now some way behind them.

Rosh gave an involuntary shudder and turned his head away.

"Look," said Jack. He was still angry and clearly not prepared to speak to Rosh in anything more than monosyllables.

Rosh glanced ahead and saw the houses. It was a small village, little more than a hamlet. The size of the village was unimportant, however. Here they would find someone to take them back to the mainland, or, at the very least, someone with a telephone so that they could ring Jack's parents and summon the coastguard.

But Rosh, without knowing why, felt another shiver run down his spine as he looked at the village up ahead. The ground shelved steeply behind it. The houses lay beyond a field of dusty and withered-looking corn, planted in unkempt rows, at the foot of a rugged, boulder-strewn slope that was blocking out the sinking sun. Already the village was deep in shadow.

14

Children at Play

The little cluster of houses had a decidedly ramshackle look to them. They seemed to have been built from a vast collection of washed-up bits and pieces, the result of some mammoth beach-combing operation. Some of the dwellings had doors of rusted iron that had obviously once been part of the fixtures and fittings of a ship's cabin. There were round windows that had once been portholes. One house was roofed over with the curving bows of a long, wooden rowing boat. Huge, hardened globules of sea-smoothed cement were piled up to form walls. Salt-bleached planks had been hammered together to form rickety fences. They marked out the litter-strewn gardens in which a few bedraggled cabbages struggled to grow.

There was an air of desolation and emptiness about the village. But, as they walked into its shady main street, Rosh and Jack heard signs that this was not an abandoned settlement. They could hear the villagers. Or some of them.

The high-pitched voices of young children filled the air with a mixed up jumble of cries and squeals; the unmistakable sounds of a playground.

A passageway ran between two buildings. One was a lopsided bungalow with a pair of ship's lamps, one green and one red, hanging either side of the front door. The other was a two-storey building that had the look of a shop about it, though there were no goods for sale on visible display. A wrinkled canvas blind filled the inside of the large front window, blocking any view of the shop's interior. A row of dead wasps, trapped between the glass and the canvas blind, were dotted along the lower portion of the window. The sound of the children at play was coming from a passage next to the shop.

Rosh and Jack arrived at the gap between the two buildings and stopped. They looked at the group of children playing there. The youngest was a bow-legged toddler, his shorts bulging to accommodate an ill-fitting nappy. The eldest was a pale-faced girl of around seven, her hair pulled back in a severe ponytail.

"What exactly are those kids doing?" Rosh said, after watching them in silence for a few moments.

"They're just mucking about," Jack said. His recent anger with his cousin seemed to have burnt itself out. "Come on, Rosh, we need to find some grown-ups!"

"I don't like the look of it," said Rosh, still watching the children. He took a few steps towards them. None of them had noticed, as yet, that they were being observed.

There were no swings, no climbing frame, no slides. The passage was no ordinary playground. But then, the children were playing no ordinary game.

Someone had hammered a rough wooden post deep into the ground. The children were gathered around this post and, as he drew closer, Rosh could see that one of them had been tied to it. A length of blue nylon cord had been wrapped around the wrist of one grubby boy, around five years of age. His skinny arms stuck out like twigs from the folds of the enormous string vest he was wearing. The other end of the cord was fastened to a metal ring half embedded in the top of the post.

The boy in the vest tugged at the cord binding his wrist and shouted shrilly at the others to let him go. They ignored him, preferring to listen to the pale-faced girl. She seemed to be issuing instructions of some kind. Rosh could not make out exactly what she was saying from amidst the excited babble of children's voices, but it was on her signal that they all formed a circle around the skinny-armed boy and began skipping around him. As they danced and capered about, with all eyes on their captive, they began singing a rhyme in harsh, mocking tones, which they repeated over and over again.

> *"If ever we're in trouble*
> *With a snooper or a spy*
> *We all go a-wicketing*
> *And watch our troubles fly.*

A-wicketing, a-wicketing
Up on Wicket Hill
The island first, the island last,
The island for the kill!"

The children roared out the final word, "kill!" in a combined shout that echoed like a gunshot between the walls of the buildings either side of them.

The boy in the vest was tugging at the post more desperately than ever. He was red in the face and still yelling at his companions at the top of his voice. His words were drowned out, though, by the more and more frenzied chanting, which rose in volume and increased in speed, as the wild dance grew wilder still.

So intent were they on their sinister game that none of them noticed Rosh coming towards them. He stopped a few metres from the whirling dance.

Jack joined him. Glancing at his cousin, and noting the perplexed frown on his face, Rosh knew that Jack no longer thought that the children were "just mucking about". One look at the expression of the child tied to the post must have told him that. Even so, Rosh himself was finding it difficult to make up his mind whether or not to intervene.

Jack too, appeared hesitant. They both watched in fascinated horror.

The childrens' song reached a violent crescendo then stopped abruptly as the pale-faced girl raised her hand. The circling dancers tripped and stumbled into stillness, but there was no laughter. Even the boy tied to the post fell silent and stopped yanking at the cord that bound his wrist.

All eyes were on the pale-faced girl, but she still stared at the boy in the vest, drilling him with a look of hatred and disgust. He let out a low moan and slowly raised his free arm to shield his face.

The girl now led a new chant, beginning as a whisper, but rising in volume as the other children quickly joined in.

"Wicketer, wicketer, wicketer, wicketer!" they chanted, all their cold eyes fixed on the thin boy roped to the post. "WICKETER! WICKETER! WICKETER! WICKETER!" The chant rose to a deafening shout and then suddenly the children were all on their knees, snatching up handfuls of dirt, old tin cans, pieces of rubbish, and they began pelting the boy with any missile they could find. He flinched and ducked and let out a wail that was quickly drowned out by the excited squealing of his tormentors.

And *still* Rosh and Jack remained rooted to the spot. The scene was so wild and brutal that they had both been shocked into stillness. Then Pale Face herself stood up and took a step towards the cringing captive. In her raised right hand she held a stone the size of her fist.

15

A Thin, Snickering Laugh

For Rosh, it broke the spell of inaction at last. The sight of the heavy stone about to be brought down on the head of the defenceless boy, right there in front of him, shook him out of it. He felt himself move forward before he had even registered what was happening. At the same time he heard Jack react too, letting out a sudden shout of alarm, as if to warn the boy.

Immediately, there was silence. Jack's wordless

cry echoed around the passage. The children all gawped at the two older boys. The stone dropped from the pale girl's hand and thudded on to the ground.

"Spies!" she whispered, pointing a trembling finger at Rosh and Jack. "Spies and snoopers! Real ones!" and she turned on her heels with a shrill scream and ran. Then the others ran too, streaming away like a shoal of fish fleeing from the shadow of a heron at the river's edge.

Jack took one or two threatening steps after them. Rosh turned to the boy at the post. He was crouching on the ground and was once again trying desperately to free his hand, all the time fixing Rosh with a look of stupefied dread.

"It's all right," said Rosh, smiling. "They've gone."

"Yes," said Jack, turning back after his feigned pursuit and kneeling down beside the boy in the vest. "We scared off those little creeps. You're safe now." He reached out a hand, perhaps to pat the boy on the head.

"Muck off, bum-head!" The boy snarled and lunged towards Jack, teeth bared, trying to bite the older boy's hand. Jack leapt back quickly.

"Did you see that?" Jack's voice went up a couple

of octaves, full of indignation and alarm. "He tried to bite me, the little . . . After we saved him from getting his head bashed in too!"

"Get away, filthy spies!" the little boy screamed. "Me sisters and brothers'll be back in a minute and then we'll do you! We'll do the both of you!"

Jack looked down at the boy, aghast.

"You don't mean to say that those kids were your brothers and sisters?" he said.

Before Jack could say any more, however, Rosh waved a hand, warning him to silence. The passageway, already steeped in the shadows of the deepening dusk, had suddenly darkened a little further. Rosh turned around slowly. Two tall figures stood in the opening to the passage, blotting out what remained of the daylight. A man and a woman stood in silence, staring fixedly at Rosh and Jack.

Looking round to see if Jack had noticed them, Rosh saw three more people, two men and a woman, step into the passage at the other end. They sauntered towards the boys. None of them uttered a word.

The first couple also walked slowly into the passage. When they drew close, the man leant against the side wall of the shop while the woman stood with her arms folded across her chest and sullenly chewed gum. They did not take their eyes off the two boys.

Behind them, the child in the vest had at last succeeded in wriggling his hand out of the nylon loop. Rosh watched him run down the passage, taking the same direction the other children had. As he ran past the three adults, the woman raised her hand as if to slap him and one of the men aimed a kick at the boy's shins. The third adult let out a mirthless snicker.

Jack cleared his throat.

"Hello," he said brightly, addressing the couple in front of them, "I wonder if you can help us?"

"Us?" echoed the woman chewing gum.

"Help you?" added the man. He spoke softly, but there was an unmistakable air of menace in his tone. The snickering laughter came again from close behind them.

"We're surrounded," Rosh whispered to Jack.

"Don't be daft," Jack whispered back. But there was uncertainty in his voice. Uncertainty and fear.

"You been bothering our kids?" said the woman, still standing with her arms folded, still chewing gum.

"We don't like that," said the man with the soft voice.

"Didn't you see what they were doing?" Rosh spoke up, his fear lending him a certain angry defiance. "They had that little one tied up and the girl was about to . . ." But Rosh dried up as he noticed the cruel smile on the man's face. It was as if the man knew full well what the children had been doing and was enjoying hearing about it. So Rosh remained silent. Jack, however, seemed to feel he had to take up where his cousin had left off.

"He's right you know," he said. "Those kids were absolute nutters!"

There was a silence. All was still, apart from the grinding jaws of the gum-chewing woman.

"Those are our children you're talking about," the man said. His voice was softer and even more menacing than before.

"We know what you are," said the woman.

"Eh?" said Jack. His voice cracked and shot up in a high-pitched squeak. Rosh would have laughed if he had not been so afraid.

"Yes," the man said, "we know. Spies come in all shapes. Snoopers come in all sizes. And you know what we do to spies and snoopers, don't you?"

"No," said Jack. He seemed unable to stop talking. "No, we don't, do we Rosh?"

No one spoke. Behind them, once again, someone let out a thin, snickering laugh.

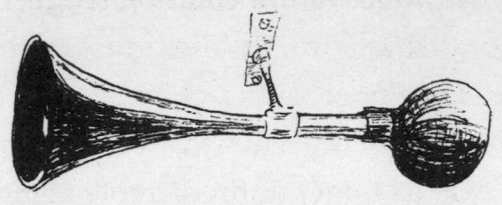

16

Weird Conveyance

There was a sudden, unexpected sound. It was the blare of an old-fashioned car horn, floating through the twilight air. The man with the soft voice exchanged looks with the gum-chewing woman. Nobody moved and nobody spoke, but nevertheless a change came over the company. The threatening atmosphere was temporarily put on hold. They were waiting for something. Or someone. Rosh and Jack had little choice but to wait with them.

The horn sounded again, a resonant honking that reminded Rosh of a performance by clowns he had seen as a small boy. It was not a happy memory. He had had to leave the circus early, feeling sick, and had thrown up in the grass outside the tent. He remembered the clowns, who were in the middle of their act when Rosh had made his hurried exit, as huge, unpredictable giants, full of menace. And now he felt as if he were back at that circus, but this time he was out in the sawdust sprinkled ring, trapped in some distorted and deadly version of the clown's frightening act.

The woman was still chewing, but now she glanced over her shoulder. There was a distant rumble and a clattering sound that filled the air, growing louder by the second. It was the sound of wheels turning, mingled with the pounding of heavy footsteps on baked earth.

A strange vehicle appeared at the top of the passage in a blaze of orange light. It turned down into the gloom between the two buildings, illuminating the scene by means of two guttering oil lamps that swung on hooks, one on each side of its curved roof. The five adults in the passageway all moved forwards but then had to back away again to allow the weird conveyance room to manoeuvre. Their shadows, stretching up as tall as the rooftops, danced and shivered across the walls on either side.

Rosh and Jack stood, seemingly forgotten. They both began to back away, surreptitiously.

"When I count to three," Jack whispered as they both edged backwards down the passageway, "we turn and run, OK? One . . . two . . . Ow!"

Jack's countdown was cut short as he walked backwards into the post that the boy in the vest had been tied to. Rosh bolted a few steps then stopped. Jack was lying where he had fallen. The woman with the chewing gum was standing over him. Rosh walked back towards them.

"You should've run," Jack said to him.

"Don't be stupid," said Rosh. But, he thought, if this had happened just a few hours ago he probably *would* have abandoned his cousin, and he wondered if he would regret this change of heart.

He remembered the sight of Jack weeping after their fight. It was a sight that had unnerved him. He had been unable to suppress a pang of remorse at the way he had behaved towards his cousin and his family. The thought struck him that perhaps he was more to blame than he had admitted for the atmosphere of strained boredom that had filled the house at Fleming.

The strange vehicle that had arrived in the passageway turned out to be a large and elaborate-looking rickshaw. It looked as if it had been made from the back half of a dilapidated vintage car, fitted on to parts of an old hay cart. As well as the two oil lamps fitted either side of the roof there was also a large brass car horn, the sort with a hollow rubber ball attached that you squeeze to make a honking sound, hooked to a bracket by the window of the passenger compartment.

Between the shafts of this bizarre conveyance stood Hobbs, a leather harness secured around his broad shoulders. He was dripping with sweat and panting hard. The rickshaw looked heavy, and he had obviously just pulled it at great speed from Blood Willow Hall down to the village.

A door in the rickshaw's passenger compartment swung open and Sir Algernon stepped out. He was no longer dressed in his black mourning clothes. Now he wore a suit of white linen. But he still carried his silver-topped cane. He rapped out an angry tattoo with his stick, battering the roof of the rickshaw. Then he glared around at the small group of people in the passageway until he was sure he had their attention.

"These two," he said, gesturing towards Rosh and Jack with his cane, "these two are coming back to the Hall for the time being."

There was a chorus of muttering from the group. Rosh heard the words "spies" and "snoopers" repeated several times.

Sir Algernon gestured angrily with his stick.

"You all know the island ways," he said. "You all know our traditions of, shall we say, hospitality. But it looked to me as if you lot were thinking of making up an unofficial welcoming committee of your own for our two guests here. Dear me. You should be ashamed of yourselves. How often do we get the chance to entertain? Once in a blue moon. Now you have something more to look forward to than herding scabby sheep and gathering winkles down on the beach. So we respect the old ways, the old traditions and the old hierarchies. When I say that these two stay in the Hall tonight, they stay in the hall tonight! Am I not the master of Blood Willow Hall? Well, am I not?" He glared at the group.

Rosh had been watching them while Algernon spoke. The villagers' expressions changed from sullen resentment to acceptance, then to genuine enthusiasm. Now they stood nudging one another in barely contained excitement.

"So, we're agreed then. We'll stick to the old ways, as I say. Tomorrow we shall show our young friends here the true meaning of island hospitality. Do I make myself clear?"

There was a murmuring of assent, and much vigorous nodding of heads.

"Very good. Now get to your homes, all of you. You'll be needing a good night's sleep. You in particular, Spindle," he said, addressing the soft-voiced man, "will need to be up at dawn tomorrow. The ground needs to be prepared," he added darkly. "Up on Wicket Hill."

The small crowd were content. They nodded some more. The soft-voiced man smiled. Someone snickered. Then they all moved away, out of the passageway.

Now Sir Algernon turned to Rosh and Jack. He pointed his cane at them.

"Rather rude of you boys," he said, "to leave without saying goodbye. We like to keep to the traditional ways here on the island, as you will discover. There is no possibility of you leaving. Get that out of your heads for good, then we can all enjoy our evening. Now, into the rickshaw with you both."

Jack climbed in through the door to the passenger compartment. Rosh swallowed, then followed his cousin into the dark interior.

"Hobbs!" Sir Algernon said, loudly. The large man started, as if he had been asleep on his feet. Algernon waved his cane shakily above his head.

"To the Hall!" he cried, throwing back his head and staggering a little giddily, his eyes fixed on the rapidly darkening sky. Then the old man bent down and climbed into the back of the rickshaw with the two boys. He slammed the door shut behind him.

17

Rescued or Recaptured?

There were no lights inside the rickshaw. They sat in the gloom, Rosh and Jack together on a double seat and Sir Algernon opposite them, leaning forward on his cane.

Outside, the desolate island landscape passed by, the trees and cliff-tops silhouetted against the inky blue sky. Inside, the passengers were jolted and jarred as Hobbs pulled the vehicle along the uneven path. The rumbling of the wheels and the incessant juddering of the whole compartment made any conversation impossible. Rosh was relieved when the rickshaw came to a halt.

"Doesn't anyone have a normal car around here?" Jack said, in the silence after the wheels had stopped turning. "This thing we're in is rubbish! I think I'm going to be sick." He groaned and held his stomach.

"Not on the upholstery, please!" Sir Algernon said. Hobbs had now unbuckled his harness and had lumbered around to open the door. Jack and Rosh clambered out unsteadily. Hobbs loomed over them, regarding them both with a doleful expression. The flickering light of the rickshaw's oil lamps played across his puckered, hang-dog features. The big man was watching them closely. There was clearly no chance for Rosh and Jack to dash away into the night. Even if the opportunity arose, Rosh was not sure whether it would be wise for them to take it. Had they been rescued from the villagers by Sir Algernon? Or had they been recaptured by him? Nothing made sense on this island.

"We really do need to find a telephone," Rosh said. "It's late. Jack's parents will be worried."

Hobbs looked blank. It was Sir Algernon,

carefully climbing out of the rickshaw, who replied.

"I'm afraid that's completely out of the question," he said. "There are no telephone lines here on the island. Just as there are no 'normal' cars. I think Hobbs does perfectly well powering my rickshaw. As for everyone else, why, Shanksy's pony is good enough for them. They walk!"

"Well, if there are no phone lines," Jack said, "surely someone's got a mobile?"

"My dear boy, I don't know what on earth you mean!" said Sir Algernon. He beamed at them, seemingly pleased at his own ignorance.

Jack stamped his foot. "Why didn't I bring mine!" he said to himself, anguished.

"It wouldn't have helped, Jack," Rosh said gently. "It would only have got ruined in the sea."

"Now, now," said Sir Algernon, waving his stick lightly in the air, "no need to take on so, Jack, old lad. I don't suppose your parents are worried. They probably just think you've drowned, or something."

Jack looked aghast. Sir Algernon burst out laughing.

"Just a joke, dear boy, just my little joke," he said. "You must spend the night here, at the Hall. There's nothing else you can do, nowhere else you can go. You saw the villagers. They are not used to strangers. Blood Willow Hall welcomes you back and offers you a roof over your heads for tonight. Bernie will be pleased. She doesn't much care for the village children, so it'll be nice for her to have some company of her own age for a change. Even if it's only for—" Here Sir Algernon broke off for a moment and coughed, as if he had accidentally said too much. "Well, you'll both be moving on soon enough, won't you?" he concluded, somewhat awkwardly.

Leaving Hobbs methodically wiping down the rickshaw with a damp sponge, Sir Algernon ushered the two boys up the stone steps and back through the carved doorway of Blood Willow Hall.

Bernie was waiting for them in the entranceway. Like Sir Algernon, she too had changed her clothes. She was now dressed in a faded blue, sleeveless dress, shaped rather like a sack, with a hole for the head and the arms. A white sash, tied around her waist, completed the outfit.

"Oh, there you are!" she said and she smiled toothily. "Hobbs made the tea absolutely ages ago. I thought it'd be a bit rude if I started without you. I'm jolly well starving now, and I bet you are too. Come on, it's set out in the old playroom!" She scampered away up the stone staircase. Rosh and Jack followed as quickly as they could. They were both very tired by now, but the thought of food spurred them on.

"I shan't be joining you for tea," Sir Algernon called up after them. "I have some reading to catch up on. Hobbs will see to your needs. I bid you goodnight!"

Rosh and Jack climbed the stairs. Below them, the old man headed through the double doors into the library, tapping his cane on the tiled flooring with each step he took. Rosh glanced sideways at his cousin. He cleared his throat.

"Er ... Jack," he said. "Sorry about ... you know ... kicking your legs out from under you and all that. I lost my temper. Couldn't help it."

Jack lowered his head and shot Rosh a look.

"Don't worry about it," he said. His voice was low, more of an awkward mumble than his usual loud and nasal tones. "I know I can be pretty annoying sometimes. Everybody says so."

Rosh cleared his throat again. "Yeah, well ... I suppose I was a bit of an old misery, back in Fleming. Sorry about that."

"OK," Jack said, looking him in the eye. "That's that then, yes?"

Rosh gave a sigh of relief. "Yes," he agreed gratefully.

They reached the first floor, but Bernie's clattering footfall on the stairs above told them that they had to keep climbing. They continued up a narrow flight of stairs, which had no ornate carvings on its banisters and only a few family portraits and old statues lining the walls. The main staircase had been dark enough, with only a series of guttering candles in brass sconces set into the wall at various intervals. The upper stairway had even fewer candles, and these were smaller and gave off a more tremulous kind of light. Rosh and Jack kept close together as they stumbled up the staircase behind the light-footed Bernie.

She was waiting for them on the second floor landing.

"Come on, slowcoaches!" she said. Her giggle floated through the air in the near total darkness at the top of the stairs. "This way!"

She turned and trotted away along a darkened corridor. The white sash around her waist was all that could be seen in the darkness, bobbing in front of them like a will-o'-the-wisp. Finally the hovering sash came to a halt some way ahead of them. Bernie threw open the door to the old playroom and the narrow corridor was flooded with light.

"Here we are!" she said.

They followed her into the room, which was lit by a chandelier fitted with a dozen misshapen and greasy looking candles. But to Rosh, the brightly-lit room felt warm and welcoming after the darkness of the stairs and corridor.

Most welcome of all, however, was the sight of a generous tea, spread out on a low table in the middle of the room. Some lumpy-looking cushions lay on the carpet. There were no chairs.

"Help yourselves," said Bernie.

Rosh and Jack sat down, cross-legged, on either side of the table and began to eat. There were crumbly slices of home-made bread, with a rather gritty texture. There were curling strips of smoked meat and a plate of rather scrawny chicken drumsticks. There were scones, generously spread with runny blackberry jam, and a platter filled with slabs of bread pudding, grey in colour, which trembled in the hand when lifted to the mouth. Rosh and Jack ate this fare in dedicated silence, then washed it down with cup after cup of stone cold tea that they poured from a large enamel pot.

Bernie, who ate very little, despite her earlier

claims to be hungry, kept jumping up and pacing around the room, trying to interest the boys in the various old toys that surrounded them and reminiscing aloud about the various games she had played there when she was younger. Neither Rosh nor Jack paid her any heed, a fact which did not seem to bother her in the least. She chatted on, her voice providing a background to the munching and swallowing and the occasional clink of teacups.

Jack was the first to feel he ought to try to make some attempt at conversation. He lay flat on his back on the carpet with a cushion under his head. All the plates on the table were empty. Rosh was finishing off the last few bites of the final jam-covered scone.

"What kind of a place is this, Bernie?" Jack said. "This island, I mean. Is it true what your uncle told us? Are there *really* no cars or telephones or anything? I mean, do you even have television?"

"Television? Yes, of course. They have one in the village. We watch it sometimes, when the generator's working."

"No mains electricity," said Rosh. "No plugs, no central heating, no electric lights." He glanced up at the candles.

"How do you get over to the mainland?" said Jack.

"Oh, we don't go there, not us children at any rate," Bernie said.

"What? But, you must go to school somewhere," said Rosh. "Surely there isn't one on the island?"

"Course not, silly. Uncle Algy gives me lessons, down in the library, and jolly boring it is too, I can tell you!"

"What about the other kids," Rosh went on, "the kids in the village?"

"Oh them," Bernie waved her hand dismissively. "No one ever bothers to teach them anything, apart from things like that stupid wicketing game they play."

"Wicketing," Rosh repeated, remembering the word from the song they had heard the children singing, "What *is* a wicketing?"

"Oh, it's just something the islanders are supposed to do," said Bernie. "It's an old custom. It hardly ever happens, really, but they teach us all how to do it, just in case. There's only a wicketing if we find a spy or a snooper or a stranger and that hasn't happened for years and years. I don't think half the villagers were born the last time they had a wicketing. I mean, no one ever comes here! The only strangers I've met in my entire life are . . . Oh!"

Bernie broke off suddenly. Her hand flew to her mouth and she stared at the two boys, her eyes wide with horror.

"Oh no," she said, her voice choked. "Surely not! . . . I hadn't thought . . . How could I be so silly? . . . Oh no! . . . Surely they wouldn't! . . . would they?"

Then she burst into tears and ran from the room.

18

A Sinister Tableau

Rosh and Jack looked at each other.

"Well, that doesn't seem very promising," Jack said.

Rosh nodded in agreement. It crossed his mind that only a few hours ago he would have been hard pressed to agree with Jack on anything at all. But this was fairly indisputable. It did not look good. Rosh lay down, like Jack, on the threadbare carpet and grabbed a free cushion to shove behind his head. Their stomachs gurgled in the quiet of the old playroom, struggling to digest the heavy and unfamiliar food they had been filled with. Bernie had rushed away, and, once again, Rosh had failed to thank her for the shoes and trousers. Still, there were more pressing things to worry about.

"This wicketing thing . . ." Rosh began.

"Yeah. Don't like the sound of it," said Jack.

They fell silent again, both of them deep in troubled thought. Their stomachs carried on a conversation. Moths fluttered at the window, pale and ghostly blurs against the darkness of the night sky, softly tapping at the glass.

Rosh looked around the playroom. It was a small attic with a sloping ceiling. Deep shelves on every wall were filled with a variety of toys and games, many of which had a homemade look about them. There was a large rocking horse, crudely carved, its face cruel and mask-like. The clown rag-doll was even more sinister. Made from filthy scraps of material, sewn together in an uneven patchwork, his leering smile was painted on to a leather disc of a face in cracked and fading colours.

"I bet Hobbs made all these things," Rosh said.

"Hmm . . . looks like he makes toys as well as he makes trousers," Jack said.

"I won't argue with you there," said Rosh. The novelty of not wanting to argue with his cousin was going to take a bit of getting used to.

Jack clambered to his feet and began examining the shelves more closely.

"A book," he said. "It's the only one. *Favourite Fairy Tales*. Looks like they fished it out of the sea. The pages are all crinkled up." Rosh heard a papery crackle as Jack opened the book. " 'Jack and the Beanstalk'," he read. "One of my favourites!"

Rosh got to his feet and joined his cousin in front of the shelves.

"We're stuck here for the night, aren't we," he said.

Jack gave a brief nod. There was a silence. Jack coughed and then began studying the shelves once more.

"Look at this globe," he said, sending the miniature world spinning around. "It looks like Hobbs made it out of an old marker-buoy."

The buoy had been fixed on to a rusty iron axle. The islands and continents of the earth had been painstakingly cut out of an old atlas and glued on in the appropriate places.

Rosh looked at the globe. "Where's Sri Lanka?" he said.

"That's where your mum comes from, isn't it?" said Jack, turning the buoy around until he found India. "It's here, this island next to India. Didn't you know?"

Rosh squinted at the globe.

"That's not it," he said. "It says Ceylon."

"Ceylon's what Sri Lanka used to called. Hobbs must have cut up an out-of-date map. Don't you know anything about the place?" Jack sounded surprised.

"Mum never talks about it," said Rosh.

"Doesn't she ever go back, to visit her family or whatever?"

"No."

"Oh," said Jack. He wore a puzzled frown.

"There is one thing I remember Mum saying," Rosh said. "She said they call Sri Lanka the tear drop of India."

"Yes," Jack nodded. "That's because of the shape of the island." Rosh touched the tiny, tear-shaped island, pasted on to the marker-buoy globe, and traced its outline with the tip of his finger.

"I think my mum's got sad memories of Sri Lanka," he said. "Her parents were killed when she was quite young. Something to do with a war over there. I don't really know. She never talks about it."

"But haven't you ever wanted to find out about it for yourself?" Jack asked.

Rosh thought.

"I dunno," he said, at last. "I think I was worried about upsetting Mum. She acts as if she hates the past, sometimes. She won't ever look at old photographs or anything."

"If your mum never wants to talk about Sri Lanka," Jack asked, "then why did she give you a Sri Lankan name?"

"Not even sure that it is," said Rosh. "It was Dad who picked my name. Mum wanted to call me Roger!"

"Oh," Jack said again, and he coughed.

After a few seconds' awkward pause, Rosh heard Jack suddenly draw in his breath.

"Hey, Rosh, look at this!" he said.

Jack had taken a ripped and dusty kite down from the shelf. Behind it there was a collection of carved wooden figures, each about the size of a clothes peg. They were arranged in a tableau that Rosh recognized. He had seen this game twice before, here, on this island. One figure, brandishing a round object in a stiffly upraised fist, was positioned opposite the model of a second man, who was standing with knees bent, holding up a club or bat of some kind. Red paint had been liberally applied to his head and arms. This was clearly meant to represent blood, flowing profusely from multiple wounds. All the other figures were grouped around him, their staring, painted eyes gazing avidly towards the wounded man with the bat. Behind him was a green painted disc of wood into the centre of which a tiny post had been fastened. A length of thin wire connected the carved figure to the little wooden post, one end twisted round the model's ankle, the other through a small metal eye, screwed into the top of the post.

"It's like in the painting on the stairs," Rosh said. "It's like the kids in the village. Only this time there's blood."

"You know what this is, don't you?" Jack said.

"Yeah," said Rosh. "It's a wicketing."

The two boys looked at each other.

"We have to get off this island," said Jack.

As he was saying this, Rosh held up a hand and tipped his head to one side, listening.

"Shh," he said, "I think I heard . . ." He paused. In the quiet of the attic playroom, with only the sound of the moths fluttering against the window, Rosh and Jack listened.

"Footsteps," said Jack. "Definitely footsteps. Someone's coming up the stairs."

The sound of a slow, heavy tread came closer and closer.

"That's not Bernie, is it?" Jack said.

"If it is," Rosh said, listening to the pounding steps, "then she's suddenly put on a lot of weight."

The floorboards creaked in the corridor outside the playroom.

"It must be Hobbs," Rosh said. "What does he want?"

The footsteps came to a halt outside the door. Rosh and Jack stood rooted to the spot. "Why can't they just leave us alone?" Jack said. He pointed at the door-handle. It was turning, slowly.

19
No Way Out

The door swung open. There stood Hobbs. His vast bulk filled the doorway. His expression, as always, was one of resignation and melancholy. He gazed at the two boys for a moment, blinking once or twice. Then he raised his arm and beckoned with one thick finger.

"You were right," said Jack. "Only Hobbs. I suppose we'd better go with him."

Rosh nodded.

They followed Hobbs out of the old playroom. The large man was carrying a guttering candle in a tall brass candlestick and they made their way along the corridor by its flickering light, until they came to low doorway. Hobbs pushed open the door and then stood aside. The room was tiny, with a sloping ceiling. It contained nothing except two iron beds, set side by side, with a battered wooden box in between them. The only light came from a stubby little candle on a chipped saucer.

"This is our room, is it?" said Jack. Hobbs nodded slowly.

"I suppose we'd better go in then," Jack said. Hobbs nodded again.

As soon as Rosh and Jack were both inside, Hobbs closed the door behind them. They heard a jangle of keys and the scrape of the lock as Hobbs secured them for the night.

Jack sat down on the bed.

"Well, that's it then," he said. "We're prisoners! We've been kidnapped!"

He was close to tears, Rosh could tell from the sound of his voice. But Rosh himself was experiencing again the sense of calm that had taken him over when he had thought he was going to fall from the roof of the library dome.

"At least we know how things stand now," he said, walking around the beds to the small, solitary window. "We know that Sir Algernon wants to keep us here against our will, though we don't know why . . ."

"And we don't want to find out," put in Jack, glumly.

"Which is why we have to escape," said Rosh. The window latch was rusted shut but Rosh managed to wrench it undone. The window opened inwards. Rosh tugged at it, dragging it open a little at a time. A light shower of peeling paint flecks and grains of rust drizzled down on to the floor.

"Give me a hand, will you?" Rosh said. "We might be able to climb down. Knot the sheets together to make a rope, or whatever . . ."

But Jack did not get up off the bed.

"Look," he said. There was a dull edge to his voice. He was pointing at the opened window. Rosh looked. Iron bars had been fitted across the outside of the frame, embedded firmly into the brickwork. He had been so busy struggling with the latch and the rusty hinges he hadn't noticed. There was no way out.

Rosh left the window open and lay down on his

bed without another word. The warm night air, heavy with the scent of earth and vegetation and the salty tang of the sea, filled the room. They could hear the sound of the waves beating against the island cliffs and the wind rustling through the leaves of the trees on the nearby hilltop.

They left the candle to burn itself out and then lay in the dark, surrounded by the sounds and smells of the island at night. It was a long time before either of them fell asleep.

The grey light of dawn was seeping into the room when Rosh heard something being pushed under the door. He had been asleep, he realized, though he hardly felt refreshed at all. The noise at the door woke him instantly. But before he could move he heard another, more familiar sound. The key being turned in the lock. Someone was unlocking their door and they were trying to make as little noise as possible. Still, the faint clink and scrape of metal on metal told Rosh precisely what was happening.

"What was that?" Jack sat bolt upright on his bed. Both boys had slept in their clothes, lying on the top of the itchy brown blankets. There was silence, for a moment, beyond the door, and then they heard the patter of footsteps running swiftly away down the corridor.

Rosh was the first to move, jumping up off the bed and moving over to the door. There was a slip of white paper lying on the floor. He snatched it up and crossed to the window to examine it in the early morning light.

There was something written on one side of the paper, scrawled in what looked like black crayon. Rosh frowned as he read.

YOU ARE IN DANJA – ESSCAPE WILE YOU STIL CAN.
THER IS A SEECRIT PASSIJ BEEHIND THE
FIRE PLAICE IN THE MEWSIK ROOM DOWNSTARES – JUST
KEEP GOING SRIGHT

Jack had gone to the door while Rosh read the letter. He had quietly turned the handle and was now leaning through the half-open door, looking up and down the corridor.

"There's no one about," he said, his voice quiet but full of urgency. "Let's go, Rosh."

"Look at this," Rosh waved the note in the air. Tearing himself away from the unlocked door, Jack came over to the window and looked at the paper.

"It has to be from Bernie, don't you think?" he said.

Jack grunted. "If Sir Algernon taught her to spell, he didn't make a very good job of it," he said.

"What does that matter!" said Rosh, feeling a brief resurgence of annoyance with his cousin. "What are you going to do, correct her spellings with a red pen? I need to know what you think of her plan. Should we try to find this music room, or what?'

"If this note *is* from Bernie," Jack said, "then how do we know we can trust her?"

"We don't," said Rosh, "but I don't see we've got much choice."

Jack nodded. "Let's go," he said.

20

The Harp

The corridor was as dark as ever, but they moved swiftly along. Rosh led, with his outstretched fingers sliding over the wall to guide his way. Jack followed, with one hand on his cousin's shoulder. They passed the door to the old playroom and arrived at the top of the stairs. Here some candles still burned in their sconces, so they were able to descend without fear of tripping over in the darkness.

Rosh reached up and took one of the candles.

"We might need a light in the underground passage," he explained, in a whisper.

Down in the entrance hall, morning light was flooding through the windows. There were three sets of doors.

"Those double doors lead to the library," Rosh said. "So we've got two choices. Should we split up?"

"No," said Jack. "Stick together. Come on, this door first."

The door led to a large room. The room was empty. No furniture, no carpets and nothing on the walls apart from a few dusty strings of broken spiders' web, up near the cracked plaster ceiling high above their heads.

"Nothing musical about this room," said Jack. They hurried across the bare floorboards to a door at the far end of the room, with Rosh shielding the flame of the guttering candle with his hand. This door led to another room very much like the first.

The third room was filled with what Rosh took to be large pieces of furniture covered in white dustsheets. He was about to head straight for the door when something in the shapes of the shrouded objects around them made him pause.

He lifted a corner of the nearest dustsheet to reveal carved, dark-stained wood. He gave the cloth a tug. It slid off and crumpled to the ground.

"Well, I'm not sure what that is," said Rosh, looking at the desk-sized musical instrument, with its ivory keys and ornately decorated woodwork, "but I'd say we're in the music room. And the fireplace is over there."

Rosh pointed to the ornate chimney place, with its relief figures, playing an array of ancient musical instruments, carved into the dark, stained wood surrounding the stone hearth. There was a tall mirror in a heavy frame fixed to the wall above the mantelpiece. Standing on the hearthstones in front of it, covered up with a dustsheet, was something very large indeed.

It was taller than either of them. Jack pulled the cover off. It was a heavy-looking harp and it was blocking the way to the fireplace. He tried to squeeze his way past, around the side.

"It's no good," Jack said, after a few moments' effort. "We'll have to shift it."

Rosh put down the candle, carefully, on the floor then came over to help.

"It's a spinet, by the way," Jack said. "That instrument over there is a spinet."

Rosh gave him a withering glance. "Get the other side of this harp," he said.

They began dragging the huge instrument across the hearthstones. There was a jarring squeal as the base scraped over the stone, which resonated through the harp strings, filling the room with a discordant hum.

"We'll have to lift it," said Rosh. "It's making too much noise."

"Wait a minute," Jack said, "what's this?"

There was a small wad of paper tucked into the strings near the base. He plucked it out and unfolded it.

"Another note from Bernie," said Jack. "Terrible spelling again."

"Just read it out," said Rosh.

Jack read the note aloud. " 'Passage is behind the' . . . harp that must say. 'Lift it – don't' . . . what? . . . drag it, I suppose. 'Just keep going' . . . Well, she's actually written 'keep going sright' here. What do you think she means?"

"Must mean 'right'," Rosh said. " 'Just keep going right'. Is there any more?"

"Just a bit. 'Tunnel comes out near Old Raw's grave. Climb down clive'? Cliff that must be. 'Boat hidden in rocks. Love from – a friend.' "

Jack looked at Rosh. "Well, she's certainly thought of everything, hasn't she?"

Rosh took the note from Jack and slipped it into the large pocket of his velvet trousers. He took up his position on one side of the harp and tried to find a comfortable handhold. Together they lifted it a few centimetres off the ground and then, with much puffing and panting, they staggered a couple of paces. As they stepped off the hearthstones and on to the floorboards the slight difference in ground level caused them both to stumble slightly. It was enough. The great towering harp lost its balance and began to tip over. In their alarm, they dropped it to the ground far too quickly. The edge of the base slammed into the floorboards and the harp lurched over with sickening speed and fell on to its side.

In the silence of the old house, the harp hit the floor with a noise like an explosion. As the echoes reverberated, all the harp strings, from the thickest, deepest tone to the slenderest, high-pitched note, hummed together, like a swarm of demented bees. Rosh's candle fell one and caught the edge of a dustsheet. Flames were soon licking over the dry, white cloth.

For a second, the two boys stood transfixed. Then Jack made a bolt for the chimney place.

"Let's go!" he yelled as he ran.

Rosh rushed blindly after him, heading straight for the darkness of the great fireplace into which his cousin had disappeared. He ducked instinctively as he dashed under the fire-blackened lintel and bent down lower still as he sensed, rather than saw, the opening to the passageway in the sooty darkness.

The tunnel was very dark. Rosh stumbled down a short flight of stairs and ran along a narrow passageway with his arms stretched out in front of his face. He could hear Jack's uneven tread just in front of him. His cousin kept spluttering and gasping in the darkness.

"Spiders' webs!" Rosh heard him say, his voice faint with disgust. "I keep running through them. I've got a mouthful of spiders now. Ugh!"

The floor of the tunnel began to slope upwards and the roof got lower. They struggled on, bent almost double, then fell to their knees and crawled. Rosh was struck by the horrible thought that this tunnel might not lead back to the surface. What if it just gets narrower and narrower, he thought, and lower and lower, until we're trapped for ever in the suffocating darkness of the earth?

But then, just as it seemed Rosh's fears might be

coming true, with the tunnel roof at its lowest and the darkness at its most intense, the passageway turned a corner and they found themselves in a high-vaulted cavern. Quite how high it was they couldn't tell, because they were still in total darkness, but Rosh was glad of the chance to straighten his back. He felt his way forward. He found another tunnel entrance a little way in front of him, and stumbled in.

A breath of air wafted down the tunnel, bringing with it the scent of the sea. Rosh breathed in deeply. It was then that he noticed the smell of smoke drifting up through the stale air of the secret passageway. He turned and stared back into the darkness, remembering the fallen candle and the flames flickering over the dustsheet. Blood Willow Hall must be on fire.

21
Flies in a Web

"Rosh, the tunnel carries on over here!"

Rosh heard Jack's voice from somewhere away to his left.

"Can you smell the smoke, Jack?" he called back. "The Hall must be on fire!"

"Yes. I wish we'd brought that candle with us instead of starting a fire with it. I can't see a thing. Still, if Sir Algernon and his friends from the village are after us, perhaps it'll slow them down."

"What should we do? About the fire?" Rosh said.

"Do?" said Jack. "What do you mean, do? There's nothing we can do. We have to escape."

"But what if the Hall burns to the ground? What if Bernie gets burnt to death, Jack?"

There was a silence for a moment, then Jack said, "I think she'll be OK. Someone must have heard the harp falling down. They'll be able to put the fire out before it gets going. But don't worry about that. We have to escape."

Jack's voice was growing increasingly distant and muffled. "Jack? Where are you?" Rosh called out, suddenly alarmed.

"Hello?" Jack shouted from far away, somewhere out in the darkness. "Rosh, stay where you are! I think I've gone the wrong way. We must be in two different tunnels. Hold on a moment!"

"Over here!" Rosh yelled into the dark. "I'm here, Jack. Here!" There was a moment of thick silence in the solid blackness of the passageway. Rosh could hear his heart thumping in his chest. He didn't want to be lost here, deep underground, blind and alone.

He gave a sigh of relief when he heard the shuffle of footsteps nearby.

"Jack?"

"Here, Rosh."

The sound of Jack's nasal voice was more welcome than Rosh would have believed possible.

"You know back there, where the tunnel gets very tall all of a sudden?" Jack said. "Well, how did you get from there to this tunnel here?"

"I just sort of walked across until I felt the new entrance way," Rosh said. "What are you getting at?"

"I kept to the wall. I couldn't get rid of the feeling that there might be a great big hole in the floor."

Rosh gulped.

"I didn't think of that," he said.

"Well, it's a good thing you didn't," said Jack. "This must be the right-hand tunnel. Remember what Bernie's note said? Keep going right. The way out must be up ahead. Come on."

They stumbled on, side by side in the pitch black, for several minutes.

"Do you really think Bernie'll be OK?" Rosh said. "The smoke smell's getting stronger."

Jack ignored the question. He grabbed Rosh by the sleeve and shook his arm.

"Look!" said Jack. "Daylight!"

Rosh held his hand out in front of him. A faint glow outlined the silhouette of his five fingers. Jack was right. It *was* daylight. They had to be close to the end of the tunnel.

A few minutes more, spent shuffling through the gradually decreasing gloom, brought them to the source of the light. An ill-fitting rectangular doorway had been set into the rocks. Daylight filtered in through the gaps all around it.

"Bit weird, isn't it, having a secret entrance end in a proper door like this? I thought it'd lead to a cave down on the beach or something."

"I don't care what it looks like," said Jack, "as long as it's the way out."

He gave the door a push. There was a creaking sound and the hiss of dislodged grains of sand running down the back of the door.

"It's stuck," Jack said. He put his shoulder to the door. Rosh joined him. After a few minutes of fruitless grunting and heaving, Jack said, "Right. On a count of three, we both give it one almighty shove. One, two . . . THREE!"

Both boys threw themselves at the doorway. With a sharp crack, the door suddenly flew open. Rosh and Jack fell straight through.

Blinded by the sudden, unaccustomed light and with his limbs flailing at thin air, Rosh felt himself plunge downwards. He did not have far to fall, however. With a sickening jolt, he slammed into the hard and uneven ground and lay still for several seconds, trying to regain his senses. He quickly became aware that something was very wrong. Instead of rocks and sand beneath him, he felt polished floorboards, lumps of carved wood and what seemed to be a great mesh of wires. And, instead of the sound of gulls screaming in the sky he heard the clamour of broken harp strings, now even more discordant and muted in tone. He heard Jack groaning beside him. Rosh opened his eyes and blinked.

He lifted his head, rubbing his bruised forearms and coughing, and looked around through streaming eyes. Somehow, they had returned to where they had started. They were back in the music room.

But the room they had left barely fifteen minutes before was now a shambles. The harp lay on its side with Rosh and Jack spread-eagled on top of it, tangled in its strings like a pair of enormous flies caught in a web. Parts of the harp's great curving structure were blackened and scorched. The spinet had been reduced to a heap of charcoal. A double bass, its body cracked and its neck broken, lay on its back, smouldering and emitting plumes of grey smoke. Around the walls, a few instruments still stood, hidden under dustsheets that were now spotted with ash. The floor was awash with sooty water and there were a number of buckets scattered about. Clouds of smoke still hung in the air like an indoor fog, but the fire appeared to be out.

So Jack had been right. Roused by the sound of the falling harp, the occupants of the Hall must have discovered the fire and put it out.

But if Jack had been right about the fire he had been wrong about which tunnel they should have taken. Rosh realized what must have happened. Bernie's eccentric spelling had led them to take the right-hand tunnel where she had actually meant them to go straight on.

Rosh heard his cousin give another groan and heave himself up on to his elbows.

"That spinet's totally ruined!" Jack said, vaguely. He was obviously still half-stunned.

"I'd have to agree with you there, old thing," came a genial voice from behind them.

Rosh and Jack both turned, slowly and painfully, to face the fireplace. Sir Algernon was standing in front of it, a dustsheet draped around his shoulders, a cloud of dark smoke floating ominously above his head, a smile playing about his features.

"Do either of you lads play cricket?" he said.

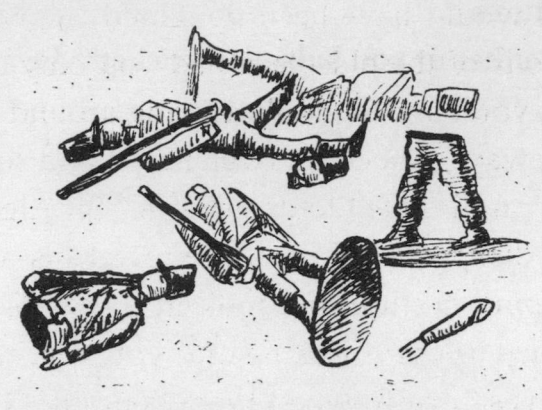

22

All Broken

"It's an interesting fact," Sir Algernon went on pleasantly, not waiting for an answer, "that the origin of the game now called cricket was invented by an ancestor of mine. Of course, you won't find that in any of the official histories of the sport, but it's well-known in these parts." His smile dropped and he adjusted his half-moon spectacles before abruptly changing the subject. "It was very poor form of you both to go poking

142

around exploring the Hall on your own," he said, "I would have been delighted to give you a full tour of the old place had you only asked. But no, you have to go blundering around secret passageways, knocking over harps and leaving lighted candles next to dustsheets." Sir Algernon gave a disapproving tut and moved his arm in a sweeping gesture that took in the whole fire-blackened room. "The results you can see for yourselves." He frowned then went on. "I am a little puzzled as to how you knew there was a secret passage in the music room, but we'll let that go. I think you two had better come to the games room. Seems we need to keep an eye on you until it's time. I'll lead the way. Hobbs will bring up the rear. I want to check up on Henry first. He's in the library." And he shuffled over to the door, calling out for Hobbs in a loud but querulous voice.

"What did he mean, 'until it's time'?" said Jack. "And what's Henry doing in the library?"

Rosh let both questions hang, unanswered, in the air. Hobbs had arrived. If he had any intention of helping them out of their predicament, it was not apparent from his dull and mournful expression. He appeared to be utterly loyal to Sir Algernon. Once again, it seemed they had no choice but to obey the old man.

In the library, the air was rent by blood-curdling shrieks. As they followed Sir Algernon into the huge circular room, the origin of the fearful noise became apparent. Henry the vulture was wheeling around the inside of the great glass dome. Rosh could feel the ripples in the air as its huge wings beat up and down. The library floor, the table and some of the large volumes that lay open upon it, were spattered with enormous bird droppings.

"Henry's not too keen on the smell of smoke," said Sir Algernon. Up in the dome, the vulture uttered a harsh and protracted scream, as if in agreement with his master. The old man glanced upwards, a doubtful expression on his face.

"I think we should probably leave him to calm down of his own accord, don't you?" he said. "I get the distinct impression he wants to be alone."

Algernon led them out of the library, but his anxious attention was still fixed on the demented bird circling the dome. He did not notice as Hobbs strode in front of Rosh and surreptitiously held out a hand-written note behind his back.

Rosh's first instinct, once he had got over his

momentary surprise, was to try to take the note. Hobbs, however, hung on to it, keeping the paper clamped firmly between finger and thumb. Rosh, it seemed, was supposed to read it, rather than take it. Hobbs glanced back, once, over his mountainous shoulder, a look of mournful urgency in his eye.

Rosh read the note as he walked along behind the large man. It was written in the same wax crayon scrawl as before.

> DON'T WURRY. I WILL THINC UP A NEW PLAN.
> GO WITH ALGERNON FOR NOW.

This time the note was signed:

> LOVE FROM YOUR FRIEND – BERNIE

Hobbs glanced over his shoulder again with an enquiring look in his watery eyes. Rosh nodded quickly, to show he had read the note. Hobbs crumpled it in his huge fist. He slowed to let Rosh walk in front again.

By this time they had passed through a number of rooms, the furniture draped in the usual dustsheets. They arrived in a room dominated by what Rosh at first took to be an enormous billiard table.

"Here we are," said Sir Algernon, "the games room!"

He crossed the floor and began rummaging through the contents of a tall cupboard. Hobbs took up station in front of the door.

Rosh and Jack waited by the table. It was not a billiards table. A miniature landscape had been laid out over it. There were tree-lined fields, green painted hillocks, a number of winding roads and a gently curving river, the banks built up either side to create a channel which contained real water. There were model buildings too, a church, some farmhouses and a windmill. The buildings were all in rather poor condition, however, with holes torn through their cardboard walls and scorch marks where attempts seemed to have been made to set them alight.

Lined up along one side of the layout was an army of model soldiers. The crude wooden figures, painted in garish colours, were set out in companies, each with their own paper flag flying over them. There were cannons too, pulled by wooden horses, or set up, ready to fire, with artillery-men grouped around them.

"I see you're admiring my war-gaming table," Sir Algernon said, emerging from the cupboard dragging a heavy wooden box. "That's my army, there. Hobbs's men are lying in those fields to the right of the windmill. We're waiting for him to make up a new batch of soldiers before we can have another game."

A heap of wooden soldiers were piled together in the field. They were all broken. Heads had been snapped off, arms and legs lay scattered about.

"Hobbs isn't really very good at war-games, are you, Hobbs? No head for strategy or tactics," Sir Algernon said. "Now, make yourself useful and come and pick up this box, there's a good chap."

The old man turned back to the cupboard and stuck his head in it. His voice became rather indistinct.

"I'm sure they're in here somewhere ... they must be ... don't want to have to use the ones in the trophy room ... Aha!"

He emerged, panting, with two large curved bats, a little like hockey sticks, one held in each hand. He laid them carefully on the floor, then turned back to the cupboard. There was a shiver of clinking iron links as Sir Algernon dragged out some lengths of thick metal chain and dumped them down beside the bats.

"Chains and bats, boys!" he said. "We don't need much else. It's time you joined in with one of our island's oldest traditions, our welcoming ceremony for snoopers and spies. It's time," and here Sir Algernon paused, a horrible smile playing about his lips, "it's time for the wicketing!"

23

To Wicket Hill

"Keep a close eye on these two, Hobbs," said Sir Algernon, "or I'll know the reason why!"

Hobbs laid a heavy hand on Rosh's shoulder. With the other he grasped Jack by the collar. He had already loaded the equipment, which Sir Algernon had dragged from the cupboard, on to a small trolley. This he manoeuvred out of the games room with his foot, while keeping a firm grip on the two boys. As usual, Sir Algernon led the way.

"Hobbs!" Rosh said, in an urgent whisper. "Hobbs! You're on our side really, aren't you? I mean, you showed me Bernie's note and all, so you must be on our side, yes?"

Hobbs made no response. His large, melancholy face gave nothing away. His hold on Rosh's shoulder showed no signs of relaxing.

As they were marched across the entrance hall and out on to the front steps, Rosh looked around, desperately hoping to see Bernie giving them the thumbs up or an encouraging smile to show she had thought up a new rescue plan. He was still not sure what the wicketing actually was, and what part he and Jack were supposed to play in it, but from all he had seen and heard, it seemed like a ceremony they would do very well to avoid. And yet Bernie was nowhere to be seen. As for Hobbs, it was impossible to tell if he could be trusted to help them or not.

As they emerged from Blood Willow Hall and descended the stone stairway, a burst of harsh cheering broke out. Some of the voices were raw and booming, others high pitched and over-excited. Rosh felt his heart sink as he saw the small crowd that was gathered around a hay-cart down on the dirt path. It was made up of the people from the village, adults and children, their eyes glittering madly and their mouths curved into vicious-looking smiles. One of the men let out a familiar, snickering laugh.

Jack, who had maintained a gloomy silence since Sir Algernon had caught them in the burnt-out music room, now let out a groan.

"Not them again!" he said.

The little crowd parted as Rosh and Jack were pushed up on to the cart. They stood clinging to the wooden rail that ran round three sides of the open-backed wagon. Willing hands amongst the crowd loaded the box, the bats and the chains on to the cart with them.

Then a whispered chant began to gather, like the sound of the wind rustling through dry grass.

"Wicketer, wicketer, wicketer!" the crowd chanted softly.

But Sir Algernon raised his silver-topped cane and they fell silent. Everyone looked expectantly at the old man.

"Onwards," he shouted, "to Wicket Hill!"

Once more the ragged, hungry cheering broke out. Hobbs got between the shafts of the cart, lifted them and set off along the path with the people capering all around in an excited throng.

Sir Algernon, at the head of the procession, swung his arms and raised his cane skywards like a drum-major leading a military band.

The cart lurched and bumped over the rutted path. Rosh and Jack hung on to the rail and struggled to keep their footing. Their ears rang from the mocking yells of the islanders. A cloud of grey dust and grit, thrown up from the path by the cart's wheels and the pounding of feet, left them with streaming eyes, unable to see.

But, despite all this, Rosh knew where they were going. He recalled the flat-topped hill that he had seen the day before, with its crown of twisted trees. It was the only hill on the island; it had to be Wicket Hill.

The ground began to incline steeply beneath the jolting cart. The islanders, still roaring and braying, seized hold of the cartwheels or grabbed on to the shafts to help Hobbs heave the wagon uphill. Sir Algernon, however, hopped up on to the cart next to the two boys, with a surprising display of agility.

"Oh, there's nothing like a good wicketing," he said, "to make a chap feel young again!"

Rosh was blinking and wiping his eyes on his sleeve. He could hear Jack coughing and spluttering beside him. He must have got a mouthful of dust.

"Nearly there, boys!" Sir Algernon called out cheerfully, as if he were some benign old uncle, taking them on a fun-packed outing to the seaside.

The ground levelled out and the cart juddered to a halt at last. As the dust settled and his vision cleared, Rosh saw that they had arrived on the flat ground at the top of the hill. A field of close-mown grass surrounded by a single row of trees, stretched out in front of them. In one corner a large and droopy-looking tent had been put up. The flaps were open at the front and Rosh could see trestle tables, piled with food, had been set up inside. In the opposite corner of the field there was a small wooden shed.

Sir Algernon stepped down from the cart.

"Hobbs!" he called. The big man was still standing between the shafts of the cart, his shoulders heaving as he struggled to recover his breath.

"Be a good lad and pop back to the Hall, would you. I forgot to let Henry out and you know how he loves a wicketing."

Hobbs turned, his face glistening with sweat, and fixed Rosh with an inscrutable look, before trudging away. Did Sir Algernon suspect Hobbs of being involved in a plot to rescue the boys? Rosh did not know. What was clear, however, was that the only person who might have proved to be an ally had been sent away. They were on their own with Sir Algernon and the islanders.

"Look at that," said Jack. His voice sounded choked. His eyes were wide with disquiet. Rosh followed the direction of his gaze and saw now what at first he had failed to notice. In the centre of the grassy plateau, two wooden posts, each with an iron ring set into the base, had been hammered deep into the ground.

24

A Method of Execution

Rough hands seized Rosh and Jack and they were half marched, half carried across the newly-mown grass, over to the two posts. The white-faced girl they had last seen in the village brought the chains from the cart, dragging them over the ground and then jangling them gleefully in the boys' faces. Spindle, the man with the soft voice, fastened the chain-links through the iron ring on each post. Then, from a sack he was carrying, he produced two shackling irons and a small hammer. Rosh and Jack were each tethered to a post; the irons fitted around one ankle and then fixed to the end of the chains, with the links hammered firmly back into place. Now there was no chance of escape.

Spindle worked swiftly, humming tunelessly to himself all the while. The woman with the chewing gum stood and watched, her arms folded and her jaws still working up and down. Rosh found himself wondering, dully, whether it was the same piece of gum she had been chewing since the previous evening. It probably was. After all, where would they get gum around here? She might have been chewing it for years!

Sir Algernon, who had disappeared into the back of the tent, re-emerged and sauntered on to the field. He had changed his clothes and was now dressed in a navy blue jacket with shiny brass buttons and a pair of white flannels. He wore a straw boater on his head, tipped at a jaunty angle. He waved his cane to the small crowd and they burst into spontaneous applause.

"Thank you so much," he said and the crowd fell silent. Someone had carried the wooden box and the two bats over from the cart. Sir Algernon stepped up on to the box, as if it were a speaker's podium, and cleared his throat.

"Ladies and gentlemen, boys and girls," he began, "people of the island and . . . er . . . guests," a murmur of laughter ran through the crowd as Sir Algernon gestured towards Rosh and Jack with his cane, "welcome to Wicket Hill. We are gathered here, in the time-honoured tradition of these shores, to deal with a potentially deadly threat. I know that none of you will allow the comparative youth of these two interlopers to influence you; we have our own village children as an example of how deadly the young can be. So, you will agree, I'm sure, that there can be no thought of mercy and that the two youths you see before you should be condemned to the wicketing, forthwith."

At this there was an enthusiastic chorus of "Aye!" from the islanders.

"Splendid," Sir Algernon continued. "In that case, I won't delay proceedings for too long." He paused and cleared his throat once more while the islanders shifted from foot to foot and tried to stifle their impatient sighs.

"As you all know, our little island community is a secret one. No authority has come to know of our existence since the first master of this islet, Sir Marmaduke Blood Willow – better known as Captain Slaughter, the infamous buccaneer – rashly accepted a King's pardon, had Blood Willow Hall built here on his island hideout, and then fell foul of His Majesty's laws once more. As you know, he ended up dangling from a hangman's noose. Only a handful of his kinsmen and retainers survived to eke out a living on this mist-shrouded rock, caring for his forgotten infant son of whom I am, of course, a descendant."

Unwilling to listen to Sir Algernon's speech any longer, Rosh turned to Jack. "You know what?" he whispered. "If we get out of this alive, I think I'd like to go to Sri Lanka one day. Just to have a look at the place." Jack looked at him blankly. Rosh, however, was determined not to think about what was about to happen to them. He carried on whispering. "I mean, London's my home and all that. My dad's British. This country is where I live, where I've always lived, but ... well, half my ancestors come from Sri Lanka, don't they? I'd like to find out something about them."

"I'm glad to see you're taking an interest in history, Rosh," Jack whispered back, "though I've a nasty feeling you've left it a bit late. But there's something I should probably tell you about your ancestors," Jack went on, "your British ones, anyway. Something I've only just realized—"

Jack broke off as he noticed that Sir Algernon had stopped talking and was glaring at them.

"You two boys! Quiet there!" Sir Algernon cleared his throat before continuing. The crowd surged a little closer around them, eyeing them coldly. Any further conversation was impossible.

"The sea has been good to us, over the centuries," Sir Algernon resumed. "Its fog and mist hide us from prying eyes. While shipwrecks have washed up much of what we need on our ragged shores, some amongst us ride the currents and skilfully supplement our resources with whatever they can steal from the houses and shops of the mainland. Occasionally, however, the sea brings us danger. Snoopers. Spies. Interlopers. It was for this that the wicketing was devised. If those mainlanders only knew the true origins of the game they play so sedately on their manicured pitches! For the wicketing is no game of cricket, no pastime for pampered public schoolboys and forelock-tugging rustics," Sir Algernon raised his voice to a braying shout, "the wicketing is not a sport, my friends, but a method of execution!"

The islanders roared their approval, whistling, clapping and shouting with excitement. Sir Algernon stepped down from the box. Eager hands opened it up and tipped the contents out on to the grass. A score of heavy stones, each one the size of a man's fist, all of them perfectly round, smoothed by the endless pounding of the sea against the shore, rolled out of the box and were snatched up by the islanders, adults and children alike. Sir Algernon picked up the two bats and came over to Rosh and Jack.

"Here you are, boys," he said, suddenly adopting a friendly manner, which in no way masked the threat behind his smile. "No hard feelings. You're allowed a bat each to try to defend yourself with. Use it to hit the stones away as we chuck them at you. Of course, you will tire eventually, and then . . . Well, like I say, no hard feelings and all that."

The two boys exchanged looks. The full horror of the situation was beginning to dawn on them.

"Poor old Bernie has taken it rather badly, I must say," Sir Algernon continued. "Terribly sentimental, that girl. She's back at the Hall in an awful sulk. Wouldn't even come to say goodbye. I blame the parents. Fancy giving a child a name like Bernice! And then, of course, they said they were tired of the life here and that they wanted to go and live on the mainland. Well, we couldn't allow *that*, could we? Even if it *was* my brother and his wife. They might have told *anyone* about us! Still, that's ancient history now, as they say. We'll break for the luncheon interval at twelve, if you're still around."

He walked away. Rosh and Jack stood staring silently at his retreating back. The islanders fanned out across the field, hefting the round stones, slapping them from hand to hand.

The white-faced girl held a stone in each fist. They were almost too heavy for her to lift, but she grinned nastily at the boys and started up the whispered chant of "Wicketer, wicketer, wicketer!" which ran all around.

Sir Algernon retired to the edge of the field and raised his cane. The chanting died away. When the silence was complete the old man threw back his head and roared out, "Let the wicketing commence!"

25
The Wicketing

Rosh and Jack stood with their bats raised. The chains at their ankles chinked as they shifted their feet. Spread out across the field, the islanders brandished their wicketing stones. A few had already thrown them; range-finding shots that had missed their targets. Their targets were Rosh and Jack.

"Here it comes," Rosh said, under his breath. His eyes were fixed on the snickering man, who was tossing a large stone from hand to hand and taking a dozen or so paces backwards, preparing a run-up. "Here it comes! Watch out!"

The snickering man ran in and hurled his stone straight at Jack. There was a rattle of chains as Jack jumped backwards. He parried the blow with his bat. The stone smacked against the varnished wood with a resounding crack.

"Splendid defensive shot!" Sir Algernon bellowed from the edge of the field. The snickering man cast an angry look in his direction, but Sir Algernon just smiled and adjusted his spectacles.

Rosh looked up to see another stone come looping in, spinning through the air, aimed at his head. He quickly squatted down on his haunches and the stone passed harmlessly above him.

Jack gave a yelp of alarm as a stone came hurtling in at ankle height. He took a step forwards and swung his bat at it. The stone rocketed back the way it had come, forcing two of the islanders to leap out of its way.

"Magnificent shot!" Sir Algernon clapped his hands loudly. "It's so much better when they put up a bit of a fight!" he added to his neighbour, beaming happily.

Rosh dodged an incoming stone and fended off

another with his bat. The stones were coming in thick and fast now. Both boys had to dodge and twist and parry and swing with their bats. The ground around their feet quickly became pitted and bare of grass. The chains rattled and clinked as they were dragged across the dry earth. Dust arose as the two boys jumped and slid. It speckled their sweating faces. The shouts and yells of the islanders rose in fury and the stones kept coming, with increasing accuracy and even deadlier speed.

Somehow Rosh and Jack managed to avoid serious injury, but the longer their ordeal lasted, the more exhausted they became. At last, Rosh slipped and fell heavily, dropping his bat to the ground. By now, the bat was cracked and splintered and unlikely to withstand much more of this battering. Rosh felt much the same way himself. He threw his arm across his face and waited for the blunt agony of the stones to come crashing in to finish him off. Nothing happened.

"They've stopped," Jack said. His voice was hoarse and heavy with fatigue. He too threw down his shattered bat and fell to his knees next to Rosh. They were both coated in a layer of grey dust, hands, faces, clothing and all. A dark smear of blood oozed beneath the grime on Jack's forehead.

His knuckles were raw and bleeding. Rosh looked down and saw that his own hands were in the same condition.

Wincing, he rubbed his eyes and looked across the field to where the islanders were trooping off to the refreshment tent. They formed a sedate queue and emerged, one by one, each holding a plate laden with food.

"They've stopped for lunch," said Rosh.

"It must be twelve o'clock," Jack said. He groaned and leaned his back against Rosh. "I'm sure all my fingers must be broken by now," he said.

"They'll be back after they've had something to eat," Rosh said. He spoke in a dull tone, heavy with the hopelessness of their situation. "My bat's cracked and yours is broken in half. And if they start coming in a bit closer . . ."

Rosh sat up, suddenly.

"There's Bernie," he said. "I just saw her! Over by that little shed."

"Where? Where?" Jack was up on his knees.

"Don't let them know we've spotted her," Rosh warned. "We mustn't give her away. She's ducked down amongst the trees."

Jack sat down again.

"Let's hope she hasn't just come to say goodbye," he said, dolefully.

The minutes dragged by. Rosh and Jack sat, back to back, watching the islanders eating their lunch. The children were sitting on the floor. The toddler in the nappy held a sandwich in both hands and smeared it around his face. The pale-faced girl was holding the boy in the vest by one ear and yanking at it viciously. The adults stood around chatting, ignoring his yells of protest. Sir Algernon circulated amongst them, his wheezy laugh ringing out from time to time. He was holding a cobweb-covered bottle in his hand from which he poured out generous measures into the enamel mugs they were all holding. All the while, the piles of food on their plates grew smaller and smaller. Lunch would soon be over.

There was a rustling in the undergrowth at the edge of the field and a small stone came thudding into the ground by Rosh's feet.

"Don't tell me they've started already," Jack said, looking round the empty field.

"It wasn't them," Rosh said. "It's a piece of paper scrunched around a stone," He snatched it up and unwrapped it, keeping the paper carefully shielded from sight, behind his body.

"Is it a note?" said Jack. "Is it from Bernie?"

Rosh pressed the paper flat on the ground, hidden, close to his side. He read what was written on it, and then screwed it up into a ball and put it in his pocket. Jack looked at him.

"It's not just a note to say goodbye, is it?" he said. "Please tell me it's not!"

"No," said Rosh. "No, it's not. Bernie's got a plan."

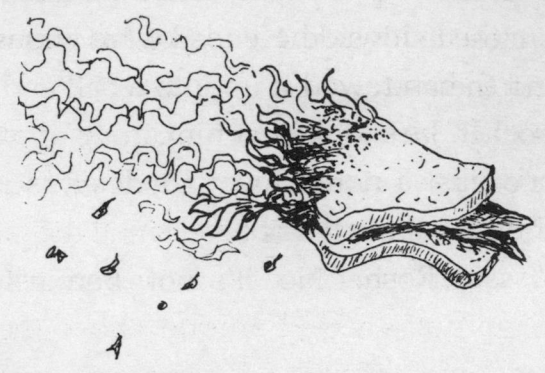

26

Sandwiches of Fire

Jack nudged Rosh and they both fell silent. Sir Algernon was strolling across the field towards them. He was carrying a plate.

"Mustn't forget about our guests," he announced as he arrived at the chaining posts. He proffered the plate, on which two sandwiches lay, their corners curled up to reveal grey, sweaty-looking slices of meat.

"No thanks," said Jack. Rosh just shook his head.

Sir Algernon shrugged and was about to turn away when he stopped and looked up. He smiled and smoothed down the ends of his moustache with his free hand.

"Splendid!" he said. "Henry's joining us at last!"

A shadow passed over them. They felt the down draught from beating wings and smelt the familiar stench of rotten meat, wafted in on the disturbed air. The vulture wheeled around above the field before landing clumsily on the grass a few metres away. He shook his greasy feathers and fixed Rosh with what seemed like an unpleasantly meaningful stare.

Meanwhile, the islanders had put down their empty plates and were advancing over the grass, stooping to pick up their discarded stones as they came. The wicketing was about to recommence.

Spindle was striding at the head of the crowd, a cruel smile on his face. But then he stopped and looked puzzled. There was a fizzing sound, like static from a broken radio. The sound grew louder and louder.

The islanders all stopped in their tracks and exchanged looks. Sir Algernon was staring at the little wooden shed on the far side of the field.

Clouds of orange smoke were billowing from the gap above the ill-fitting door.

"What the blazes . . .?" he began.

The air was rent apart by a thunderous explosion. The shed flew apart, consumed by a ball of flame and smoke. From the midst of this fireball, flaming missiles lanced out in all directions, some shooting across the ground, others arching into the trees or blasting straight upwards into the sky, exploding at a great height in a burst of coloured sparks.

Sir Algernon stood transfixed, the plate of sandwiches still held in his hand, as a burning rocket shot straight towards him. The rocket struck the plate, smashing it to pieces. With a yell of terror, Sir Algernon threw himself flat on the ground, landing on the grass in a shower of broken crockery.

One of the sandwiches was vaporized in an instant but the other went sailing through the air, burning fiercely. The blazing bread struck the gum-chewing woman on the shoulder. She shrieked and beat out the flames as she ran for cover.

Henry launched himself into the air with a squawk of dismay and flew blindly straight into Spindle, who was thrown backwards on to the pale-faced girl. They all fell, in a wild tangle of arms, legs, wings, claws and stinking feathers, down on to the scorched grass while the air above them was filled with explosions of coloured fire.

Rosh and Jack, who had instinctively crawled as far away from the erupting shed as their chains would allow, lay on their bellies and covered their heads.

A new frenzy of sizzling caused Rosh to look up. What remained of the shed was now aglow with the fierce white light of burning magnesium. He looked away, the light too intense to bear. It was then that he saw her, fearlessly running towards them across the scorched grass, her home-made dress flapping around her skinny frame like a potato sack tied to a stick; it was Bernie.

She knelt down beside them.

"Hello, you two," she said as she struggled to catch her breath, "time to go, I think." She waved away the thick tendrils of smoke that were swirling around them, and stood, grinning and blinking. "Hobbs is rather good at making fireworks, don't you think? We usually let them off on the same night as the Fleming Regatta, otherwise someone on the mainland might notice. Still, I don't suppose it matters just this once. After all, it is during the daytime and the fireworks probably won't show up that much." Bernie put her hand to her mouth and coughed. "Well, come on then! This smoke won't last for ever you know," she concluded.

The whole field was lost in the smog. Sir Algernon and all the islanders had fled, although some shouts and some fits of coughing, coming from the direction of the shed, showed that one or two of them were probably attempting to put the fire out. If there was an ideal time for escape, it was now.

"Haven't you forgotten something?" said Jack.

"We're chained up!" Rosh said, shaking his leg to make the chain-links jangle.

"Oh bother!" said Bernie. "Wait there," she added. She turned and disappeared into the bank of thick smoke that still surrounded the field.

Half a minute later she was back, with the hulking figure of Hobbs lumbering at her side.

"Hobbs'll help," Bernie said, "but he wants to hear both of you promise not to tell anyone about the island. Do you promise?"

"Yes!" said Rosh and Jack together. Hobbs just stood there, immobile, gazing down at them through mournful eyes that did not blink once, despite the smoke-filled air.

"Say it, then," said Bernie. "Hobbs may be willing to defy Sir Algernon at times, but he won't let anyone betray the island. He has to hear you promise."

"OK. We promise not to tell anyone about this island," the boys spoke together, in a rapid chant.

After a second or two, Hobbs gave an almost imperceptible nod of satisfaction and moved over to the chaining-posts. He wrenched them out of the ground as if they were twigs in sand. He handed Rosh and Jack their respective posts.

Hobbs and Bernie led the way through the smoke to the shelter of the trees. Here Hobbs knelt down and prised the irons off the boys' ankles with his bare hands.

They headed down the hill and then struck out across country, heading for the cliffs where Rosh and Jack had first come ashore. Hobbs kept his eyes on the ground. Bernie chattered away, reeling off the details of various games she had played near certain clumps of bushes or wild flower patches as they passed them by. Rosh and Jack kept glancing back, fearfully, towards the hillside, which now resembled a miniature volcano, with its crest buried in a pall of smoke.

27

Clear of the Island

Nobody appeared on the smoke-shrouded hillside to give chase.

"They probably won't even notice you're gone until they've put the fire out," Bernie said. "After all, they think you're chained up." She gave a quick giggle. "Magnesium's awfully difficult to put out once it's on fire, so you don't have to worry."

"What about you?" said Rosh. "Won't you and Hobbs get into trouble for helping us escape?"

"I suppose Uncle Algy will probably get a bit cross," Bernie said. "But I won't get sent to the wicketing like you two were, if that's what you're thinking. Hobbs would never let anything like that happen to me. He puts up with a lot, does Hobbs, and he is awfully loyal to Uncle Algy, despite everything. But as you can see, there are some things even *Hobbs* won't stand for and then there's no arguing with him. I shall probably just get sent to my room for the evening or something. Or Uncle Algy might just let me off altogether. He does rather spoil me sometimes. Maybe he feels guilty for getting rid of my parents."

Rosh and Jack stared at her, dumbfounded.

"You *know*?" said Jack.

"Oh yes," Bernie said nonchalantly. "But it happened so long ago, back when I was a baby, I don't remember them or anything. Hobbs has always looked after me. And Algy, of course. I suppose they've been like a mum and dad to me in a way." She giggled lightly at the thought.

"*Hobbs* looked after you?" Rosh glanced at the huge, silent man lumbering along beside them. "I've never even heard him speak," he whispered to Bernie, "I didn't know he could."

"Oh, Hobbs can speak, all right, can't you,

175

Hobbs?" said Bernie. "He just doesn't do it very often, that's all."

Hobbs inclined his head very slightly, the only sign that he had heard anything of the conversation.

By this time they had arrived at the cliff-top and were standing on the shingle-strewn slope above the series of rocky ledges that led down to the sea.

"The boat's down there," said Bernie. "It's tied up by the rocks, just where the water gets deep. Watch out for Uncle Algy's shark." Then she turned to Hobbs.

"Have you got that bread?" she asked him. Hobbs produced a squashed and grubby-looking loaf from his jacket pocket. He shuffled to the cliff edge and began tearing off lumps of bread and hurling them high into the air. In no time there was a flock of sea birds wheeling and screeching above his head. They were the same vicious, yellow-eyed creatures that had attacked Rosh when he first climbed the cliff. Now they were swooping and diving acrobatically to catch the pellets of bread that Hobbs was throwing to them.

"It's safe to climb down now," Bernie said.

She walked with them to the first ledge.

"Why did you do it, Bernie?" Rosh said. "Why did you help us escape?"

"Because I didn't want you to be killed, of course!" she said. "You're both much too nice to be wicketed."

"But don't *you* want to leave, too?" Rosh said. "I mean, you could come with us now, escape from here!"

"But this is my home," said Bernie. There was a rather indignant tone in her voice. "This is where I live!"

"But the people here!" Jack said, "and your Uncle! I mean, of all the absolute nutters I've come across he really is . . ." He trailed off when he noticed Bernie's expression. "But you're right, of course," he said with a shrug. "It's a family thing."

Bernie considered this. "We *are* a little family, Hobbs and Uncle Algy and me. And I really don't think we'd fit in anywhere else."

Rosh looked at Jack, who gave another shrug. They could both see that Bernie was right.

There was a pause. Rosh turned to Bernie. "Well, thanks for everything. You know, the trousers and the shoes, and everything," he trailed off.

"We owe you our lives," said Jack. His solemn tone made Bernie giggle.

"Don't be silly," she said. "Off you go now, before Hobbs runs out of bread. I'll tell Uncle Algy you promised you wouldn't tell anyone about the island. He sets a lot of store by that sort of thing. A gentleman's word is his bond, and all that."

"Yes," said Jack, "tell him that he has our word. The word of the Blood Willows." Jack turned away. Bernie gave a puzzled frown and looked at Rosh, but he could only shrug. Before he turned to follow his cousin, he stuck his hand out awkwardly, his eyes on the ground.

"Thanks, Bernie," he said, "and thank Hobbs for us, too."

Bernie grabbed his hand and squeezed his fingers for an instant, then she let go and Rosh was on his way. As he walked to the cliff-top he heard Bernie sniff.

"Now you've got me started," she said thickly. "I'd promised myself I wouldn't. But now you've gone and made me . . . cry!" And she burst into a loud fit of unabashed weeping.

With the sea birds otherwise occupied, the climb down to the foot of the cliffs was achieved without much difficulty. Rosh and Jack waded through the shallows to the line of surf-washed rocks. They found the boat. It was a wooden rowing boat of ancient and rather fragile appearance, but it was afloat, and two oars lay inside, resting on the wooden plank seating. They unfastened the mooring rope, which had been looped around a seaweed-covered crag, pushed off from the rocks and struck out with the oars. They headed for the bank of low mist that seemed to permanently surround the island. Once they were within the thick, rolling cloud the island became invisible to them, and they began to feel a little safer.

"We've done it, Rosh," Jack said, grinning broadly. "They can't stop us now! We've got away!"

"I won't be happy until we're back on the mainland," said Rosh, gripping the oars with his bruised and battered hands. He gazed out over the water.

"Fog's thinning out," he said. "We must be getting clear of the island." But then he gave a groan of despair. "Look who's here," he said. "And don't try telling me it's only a basking shark!"

Cutting through the waves, a grey dorsal fin had emerged from the water, with the tip of a tail fin also visible, a frighteningly long distance behind it. The shark described a wide circle around the small boat.

"Great Whites are known to sink small boats to get at the people inside," Jack said, his voice shaking. "After all we've been through, too. This just isn't fair!"

Rosh passed one of the oars over to his cousin.

"Get hold of this," he said. "If it gets too close we'll hit it with the oars. Apparently they swim off if you fight back."

"Wait a minute, what's that?" Jack said, holding up his hand. A whirring, clattering sound was filling the air, getting louder and louder by the second. A wind whipped up from nowhere, puckering the surface of the water and flattening the waves. Jack threw back his head and let out a shout of relieved laughter, which was quickly drowned out by the churning of what was now clearly the blades of a helicopter, hovering somewhere not far above their heads.

28
Blood

The helicopter was right above them. Its whirling blades seemed to push back the bank of fog. The shark sank beneath the waves. That was the last they saw of it. A rope ladder was lowered and the two boys were lifted out of the sea.

As the air-sea rescue craft swung around to head for the nearest coastguard station, one of the crew looked at the boys' damaged hands and pale, exhausted faces and shook his head.

"You lads are lucky to be alive. It's a good thing you fired off those distress flares or we'd never have found you. I don't understand why you didn't send them up earlier, you both look done-in. We've been sweeping the area for you two since last night, when you didn't come back to the beach. It's a wonder you survived for so long out here."

They all gazed out through the helicopter's side-door window. There was a momentary thinning in the banks of swirling mist that concealed Blood Willow Island, not enough to reveal the cliffs or the Hall, but they did catch a momentary glimpse of a large bird.

The helicopter crewman gave a start.

"Did you see the size of that thing down there? Black wings and a white head. What was that, an albatross?"

"It was a vulture," said Rosh. "Its name's Henry."

The man laughed.

"What do you think this is, mate, London Zoo? I may not know much about birds but even *I* know you don't get vultures in the north east of England!"

The crewman turned away. "We've got a comedian here, lads," he said to the rest of the crew.

Rosh and Jack exchanged glances.

"I'll bet that's one of the reasons no one knows about the island," Rosh said quietly to his cousin. "If anyone ever *does* catch sight of anything weird out here, they just end up not believing their own eyes."

A thought occurred to him then. "What did you mean, by the way," he said, "when you told Bernie we'd given her uncle the word of the Blood Willows?"

"Oh, yeah." Jack looked awkward. "That's what I was going to tell you, back before the wicketing got started, you know, about our ancestors. But I don't think you're going to like it."

"What are you on about?" said Rosh. "Tell me!"

"Well," said Jack, "when we first moved up here, Dad said he was sure some of our relatives had come from around Fleming, years and years ago. You know how he got into investigating the whole family tree thing? Well, I helped him with it a bit. We used to go to loads of old churches and look through the parish records and stuff like that."

"Well, what's that got to do with . . ." Rosh began, then stopped. He looked at his cousin. "Wait a minute," Rosh said slowly, "you don't mean that Sir Algernon is . . .?"

Jack nodded miserably. "Don't you remember I

said I recognized the coat of arms on the hall door? I'd seen it before, on that pretend parchment thing Dad's got hanging in the dining room. Some distant branch of the family. He had the name down as Willoe, different spelling and without the 'Blood', but they must be the same lot, what with the serpent and the circles on their shield. I bet those circles are meant to represent wicketing stones." He gave a quick shudder before continuing. "So if the Willoes are distant relatives, then the Blood Willows must be too. I didn't make the connection at first, not until I saw the hall doors again this morning, when they were taking us out to the cart." He gave another shiver and fell silent.

"Why didn't you say anything?" Rosh said. "Maybe if Sir Algernon had known we were related he might have . . ."

Jack interrupted him. "We're talking about a man who tried to get rid of own brother," he said. "I don't suppose he'd have any scruples about bumping off a few extremely distant relatives."

"I guess you're right," Rosh said.

"Who would have thought," Jack said, with a weary sigh, "that you and me would turn out to be part of a family of absolute nutters!"

Rosh smiled and sat back. The rescue crew had

wrapped him and Jack in thick blankets. He pulled his blanket up around his ears and let the droning of the helicopter blades fill his head. He was dimly aware that something had changed in the way he thought about his family, both his mother's *and* his father's side. He had a brief mental picture of them all, standing in jostling rows, stretching back into the realms of history. For the first time in his life, Rosh contemplated the past and felt curious rather than bored.

And then Jack nudged him and there was the mainland, spread out before them. They were nearly home.